Eavesdropping

"Is he asleep?" Brooke heard her father ask.

"Yes."

Brooke opened her eyes a crack. In the front seat Benji was slumped against his mother's arm. Brooke could just see the top of his head.

"About that party," said Mr. Forbes. His voice was low. Brooke strained to hear. "Maybe we should make him go. People might wonder."

Mrs. Forbes glanced up at the rearview mirror. Brooke lowered her eyelids.

"No. Birthday parties are licensed bedlam, Allen. It might trigger something. Why invite trouble? Everything's going so well. So far, anyway." She paused. "Let's just run the summer out. School starts soon enough."

"And then what?" said Mr. Forbes. "And then what?"

A Season of Secrets

Alison Cragin Herzig & Jane Lawrence Mali

AN
APPLE®
PAPERBACK

SCHOLASTIC INC.
New York Toronto London Auckland Sydney

for Peter
and for Amy

ISBN 0-590-32818-2

12 11 10 9 8 7 6 5 4 3   6 7 8 9/8 0/9

Printed in the U.S.A.   06

Acknowledgments

Our thanks to Jamie Childs and Frederic A. Webster for their willingness to share with us their firsthand knowledge of bats.

We would also like to thank Dr. Niels Low, who checked our medical facts, and Patrick H. Crossman for his invaluable deep editing.

For Margaret Gabel — and the others in Room 604 — thanks are inadequate.

About the Authors

Alison Cragin Herzig and Jane Lawrence Mali are coauthors of *A Word to the Wise* and *Oh, Boy! Babies!*, winner of the American Book Award for children's nonfiction in 1980.

They both live in New York City.

Chapter 1

"Where is he, then?" Jason asked his sister, Brooke. He bounced his soccer ball on the sidewalk impatiently. "I mean, if he's not in his classroom and he's not here, where is he?"

"There are lots of places," Brooke said. "It's the last day of school." Last day of school, she thought, first day of vacation. She felt immune to everything, irresponsible and excited, a Friday-afternoon feeling, but better, much better. It was a triple-decker Friday afternoon. An endless string of Friday afternoons. Summer. "Maybe he's in the art room collecting his pictures," she went on. "Or checking Lost and Found. Or his sneakers could have come untied. He's only six, you know. Sometimes it takes him longer."

"Not this long," said Jason. The sidewalk was buckled from the spring thaw and the ball took unexpected bounces.

1

Jason had to reach to catch it. "Everyone's been picked up already. Even the buses are gone."

Brooke looked down the street. A few empty cars were still parked in front of the school. Teachers' cars. She checked the playground again. Only the wind shifted the ropes and swings. At the far end of the ball field behind the school, some kids were chasing each other, their shouts faint in the distance.

"I'll go back in," she said. "Maybe there's someone left in the office to ask."

"I'll go," said Jason. He was already in motion. Brooke gazed after him and then stood waiting. The kids in the field had disappeared.

The front door of the school banged open and Jason came out, running. He took the steps in a leap and sprinted toward her. His soccer ball was tucked under one arm, making him look awkward and lopsided.

"Mom picked him up," he called before he reached her. "They were supposed to tell us."

"Why? What happened?"

"He got sick." Jason hesitated. "They said he fainted."

"Fainted? What do you mean?"

"I don't know. I didn't ask."

"You mean in school?"

"Yes. Sometime after lunch."

Brooke looked past him to the first grade windows on the lower floor. Brightly colored flowers and butterflies cut from construction paper had been taped to the inside of the windowpanes.

"I promised to buy him a creamy," she said.

Jason shrugged and dug at a crack in the sidewalk with the toe of his sneaker.

"Might as well go home," he said finally.

"Maybe they went to the doctor's."

"Even if they did, I'll bet they're home already," said Jason. "We'd be going out of our way for nothing. Unless you want to get creamies anyway. And bring him one."

"No. Let's go home."

"I'll race you."

"I'm not wearing my sneakers," said Brooke, "and, besides, I don't want to."

"I'd win anyway." Jason dropped his soccer ball and began to dribble and side-kick it down the hill at the start of Windrow Road.

Brooke walked slowly after him, her eyes on the ground. Windrow Road was lined with maple trees and the leaves on the overhanging branches cast shadow patterns at her feet, but she didn't notice them. She was thinking about fainting. You could make yourself faint.

She knew that because Izzy had told her. All you had to do was take twenty deep breaths, stick your thumb in your mouth, and blow hard, and you'd keel over. Guaranteed. They'd talked about doing it, to get out of a surprise quiz or a term test, but Brooke had never actually intended to go through with it. She was afraid to. Because of that time with Benji.

A long time ago. More than a year. She counted back. Last March. But she had never completely forgotten and now she remembered perfectly.

She had been doing homework in her room. Algebra. She had been doing algebra and she had to go to the bathroom. The bathroom door was closed. When she opened it, he was on the floor, not on the rug, on the tiles, slumped against the wall, absolutely still. His eyes were closed and his face was greenish white. He looked dead. She knelt beside him and took his hand, not knowing what else to do, and screamed and screamed until her mother came and carried him into his room. Her mother patted his cheeks and hands and called to him until he finally came to. His eyes had opened and after a while he seemed all right.

"He's fine," her mother had said later, after she'd taken him to the doctor to make sure. But Brooke's throat was still sore from screaming, and the marks of the bathroom tiles were still on her knees. "He just fainted," her mother said. "That's all." But still, Mom had been scared, too. She was as scared as I was, Brooke thought.

She shivered and shook the memory off. Jason was miles ahead. Brooke broke into a run to catch up. But by the time she passed the empty house on Ashpotag Road, he was already sitting on their porch railing, legs dangling, juggling the soccer ball as if he had been there all day. The station wagon was parked in the driveway.

"Beat you," he shouted.

"I said I wasn't racing." Brooke slowed to a walk to prove it. There was a blur of legs and he disappeared, the screen door slamming behind him.

Brooke followed him into the house. The front hall seemed dark, even after the shade of the porch. She stood on the worn square of oriental rug, adjusting and listening for sounds. Off to her right a cupboard door banged in the kitchen, and she heard footsteps above her head. Her mother's feet and legs and the bottom of her skirt appeared on the landing, and then the rest of her as she came quickly down the stairs. She paused and smiled when she saw Brooke.

"I'm glad you're home," she said, "Happy summer."

"How's Benji?" Brooke asked.

"Resting."

"Is he all right?"

"He's fine." Her mother pushed the sleeves of her sweater up to her elbows. "Didn't they tell you at school?"

"They said he fainted." Jason lounged in the doorway. His army fatigue jacket was unbuttoned and he had a pretzel in one hand and the open box in the other.

His mother nodded at him. "That's right. He just fainted. That's all."

"But why?" asked Brooke. "Why does he do it?"

"A combination of things," said her mother. "Fatigue. Growing pains. Overexcitement. Nothing to worry about. Where's Izzy? I thought she was coming over this afternoon to work on the ads for your job."

"Tomorrow," said Brooke. "She had to wash her hair. But, Mom, about Benji. Do other kids do it? Is it — "

"For heaven's sake, Brooke," her mother cut her off. "Stop badgering me! I told you he's *all right!* You're acting like a mother hen and I haven't got time for that now. I have to get back to school. To collect his artwork and clear out his locker. If you haven't got anything better to do, you could empty the dishwasher." She brushed past them and out the door.

"What's bugging her?" asked Jason.

"I don't get it. One little question? Honestly." Brooke heard the sound of the station wagon starting.

"Want a pretzel?" Jason offered the box.

"I think I'll go say hi to Benji."

"I need something to drink," said Jason.

Brooke tiptoed along the upstairs hall in case Benji was asleep, but he wasn't. He was on his bed, the faded blue corduroy comforter tucked to his chin. His knees were up and there was an extra pillow propped behind his head and a stack of books on his bedside table. He was reading and didn't hear her come in.

Brooke examined him for a time without speaking. The sight of the book and the top of his head made her feel better. If he was reading, he must be okay, and the top of his head looked reassuring, the same, all of his hair spiraling out from one whorl, down to his eyelashes in front and wisping over his ears at the sides. His hair was the same color as hers, a streaky brown, the color of the dining room table.

"Hi, Benj. How're you feeling? Benj?" His black sneakers hung on the two end bedposts.

"Benj!"

He raised his head reluctantly, as if he were pulling himself away from the page. Tired, Brooke recorded. His lower lip moved as he fiddled with his loose tooth.

Burrowing lower into his nest of cover and pillows, Benji considered her over the edge of the comforter. Mouse, she thought. Owl-eyed mole. Nothing different. He often looked a lot paler, really awful, especially in winter.

"Are you feeling okay?" she repeated.

Benji shifted slightly under the comforter. "I had a blood test," he said. He held out an arm to show her the small round Band-Aid.

"A blood test." Mom didn't tell me they went to the doctor, thought Brooke. "Did it hurt?"

"I don't know. I didn't look."

"Well, what did the doctor say?"

Benji cleared his throat. "He said I'm very tall for six. He said I'm growing. He said I have to take two pills now, instead of one." Benji worked his loose tooth back and forth with his tongue. "I can't swallow them."

"They're chewable," Brooke reminded him.

Benji picked up his book. "They taste like toothpaste," he said, "only worse."

Brooke pictured the pills; his "megavitamins," Dad called them. They were triangular, and even she thought they were huge, and Benji hated them. They made him gag. Nothing helped. Not even apple juice.

She turned abruptly and paced the length of his room, past his "office," the rectangular wooden box their father had made for him to play in. The door of the box was latched and padlocked. From the window, above his worktable, she looked down on the roof of the porch and across the driveway to the hedge of lilac bushes. The blossoms had gone to seed, leaving stiff, dry stalks behind. The stalks should have been clipped, but no one had done it yet. The empty house next door looked as if it were being punished for something. Brooke could see the paint peeling off the clapboards, and there was a new broken pane in one of the upstairs windows.

"Mom's gone back to school," she said, "to get your pictures."

Benji cleared his throat and turned a page.

"Have you noticed?" he asked.

"Noticed what?"

"The sign," he said without looking up. Brooke turned back to the window. The lawn around the deserted house was shaggy and overrun with dandelions. But the FOR SALE sign was gone.

Chapter 2

The house looked different with the sign gone. Less forlorn, thought Brooke, as if it hadn't done anything wrong after all. She was wondering whether it was really sold or whether the sign had been stolen, when her thoughts were interrupted by a screeching of brakes and a scraping sound from the street. Brooke switched to the front window.

"It's Mrs. Gibson," she said.

"I know. I could tell," said Benji.

"Now, stay, Delilah, stay! That's a good dog." They could hear Mrs. Gibson's commands clearly. "Stop that! Stop that nonsense! I'll just be a minute."

"Delilah's trying to get out and Mrs. Gibson's trying to stuff her back in." Brooke choked on a laugh and put a hand over her mouth.

"In the back. In the back. Lie down. Sit.

Stay." A door slammed. "All right. Good dog. I'll be back. I promise."

Brooke watched Mrs. Gibson brush the dog hairs from her sleeves and her chest and the front of her skirt and then start purposefully up the walk. She's going to barge right in and talk my ear off, she thought. She's nice, but the whole afternoon will be shot. If only Mom were here. Mrs. Gibson's head, topped with a neat gray bun of hair, disappeared from sight under the porch roof. Brooke ducked back from the window and waited. They heard the sound of a knock and the bell ringing and then Mrs. Gibson's voice from the front hall.

"Yoo hoo, yoo hoo. Anybody home?" Brooke froze where she was. She heard a rustling from Benji's bed in the corner. "Sssh," she warned, letting her breath whisper through her teeth.

"Marcie? Children? I let myself in," sang out Mrs. Gibson. "Hello. It's me, Dotty."

Brooke turned toward the door of Benji's room carefully so as not to creak the floorboards. Benji had disappeared under his comforter, leaving his book on top like a piece of debris from a shipwreck. The hallooing continued, fainter this time. She's in the living room, thought Brooke. There was a crash and the sound of things rolling. "Heaven's sakes alive," said Mrs. Gibson.

"What was that?" breathed Brooke.

"The triple tic-tac-toe game," said Benji through his cover. "A million marbles." Gusts of laughter fluttered to the top of the comforter.

"Quiet," ordered Brooke. Benji lay still.

"Where is everybody?" Mrs. Gibson hooted. Her footsteps headed toward the kitchen.

"Poor Jason," whispered Brooke. She'd forgotten all about him.

"Why, Jason Forbes, you scared me half to death. I didn't see you behind the door. I was looking for your mother. Where is she?"

Brooke heard Jason's voice. "She's not here." The voices were coming from right under her feet.

"Where could she be at this time of day?" Mrs. Gibson sounded annoyed.

"She's out."

"Oh, mercy, I hope she doesn't hear the news from somebody else," said Mrs. Gibson. "I'm going to wait. She can't be that long. You wouldn't mind, would you, dear, if I just help myself to a cup of coffee?" Jason mumbled something that Brooke didn't catch. "Now, where does your mother keep the instant?"

Poor Jason. Trapped like a rat.

"Brooke knows. I'll get her. She's up-stairs," said Jason clearly.

Creep! thought Brooke. Rotten traitor!

"Brooke! Hey, Brooke! Mrs. Gibson needs you!" bellowed Jason from the entrance hall.

Benji's fingers appeared at the edge of his comforter, followed by the top of his head and his eyes. "Don't tell her about me," he whispered as Brooke passed the foot of his bed.

Jason stood at the bottom of the stairs, jerking his thumb in the direction of the kitchen. He was grinning like a wolf. *Chicken,* mouthed Brooke. *I'll get you later.* Jason faded toward the front door.

"Jason, dear," called Mrs. Gibson, "there are marbles all over the living room floor. Would you pick them up before someone hurts themselves?"

"Ha, ha, ha," said Brooke just loud enough for Jason to hear, and grinned back at him.

The kettle was whistling in the kitchen. "Hello, Mrs. Gibson," said Brooke. "I didn't hear you come in."

"Perfectly all right, dear," said Mrs. Gibson, pouring and stirring. "I found everything myself. Have I had a day," she went on. "I'm absolutely pooped. The real-estate business is exhausting. Lucrative but exhausting."

I wonder how much she makes, thought Brooke.

"What I need is a good assistant," continued Mrs. Gibson. "How old are you now, dear? Fourteen?" Mrs. Gibson carried her coffee cup to the table.

"Fourteen and a half," answered Brooke.

"And Jason?"

"He's only thirteen."

"Too bad," Mrs. Gibson prattled on, "but be sure you come and see me as soon as you have your driver's license."

She ensconced herself at the kitchen table and drew her coffee cup toward her. I'm stuck, thought Brooke, until Mom gets back. Benji's megavitamin bottle was on the table next to the salt and pepper shakers. Brooke wondered fleetingly whether the pills came in a small size and reminded herself to remember to ask.

Mrs. Gibson was already off on another tangent, something about something.

Brooke kept her eyes on Mrs. Gibson's mouth, on her lips opening and closing, but her mind wandered off into summer. Swimming. Climbing Stark Mountain and painting with Izzy. Like last summer, only more serious. Professional. With advertisements all over town. We should raise our rates maybe, she thought.

"Brooke." The sound of her name brought her back. "Would you mind getting me an ashtray since you're up. And peek out the window, would you dear, to check on Delilah. But don't let her see you."

Brooke brought her a saucer from the drainer by the kitchen sink and then looked out to where Mrs. Gibson's Chevy was parked. The window on the driver's side was rolled partway down and Delilah had forced her head through the opening. Her tongue lolled out of her mouth and there was slobber all over the glass. Brooke had just decided not to tell Mrs. Gibson that her dumb Irish setter was strangling, when the station wagon turned into the driveway. Her mother got out with a long roll of papers under her arm. Delilah worked her head free and began to scramble from the front to the back of the car in a frenzy of barking. She lunged against the doors and pawed at the windows. Brooke watched her mother cut across the lawn, without a glance in Delilah's direction.

"Mom's back," she said to Mrs. Gibson.

"Hello, Dotty," called Mrs. Forbes through the kitchen doorway. "I'll be down in a second. Make yourself a cup of coffee."

"Delilah's fine, Mrs. Gibson," said Brooke.

When her mother reappeared she was minus the roll of papers.

"Sit down, Marcie. Have I got something

to tell you," Mrs. Gibson greeted her. "I've hardly said a word till now, but I'm bursting with news."

I'm off the hook, thought Brooke. I can call Izzy.

"Don't go, Brooke. You'll want to hear, too. It concerns our whole street." Brooke turned back and opened the dishwasher. She began to unload the dishes. Delilah was barking again.

"Tell us." Mrs. Forbes leaned against the counter, her feet crossed.

"Well," Mrs. Gibson blew into her coffee and took a sip.

There was a heavy knock on the back door.

"You won't believe this," she went right on, "but. . . ." She paused reluctantly as Sam Renwick's bulky figure appeared in the kitchen. A carpenter's apron was tied under his stomach. Hammers and pliers and other tools hung from loops in the apron, and Brooke knew that the pouch in front was full of nails. She had seen him often enough, inching across a steep roof of one or another of the houses her father was building, his feet braced against a two-by-four, hammering each shingle with six sure strokes, three to a nail.

" 'Lo Marcie, Dotty. Hi, gorgeous." He beamed at Brooke. His chin broke into creases when he smiled and his cheeks looked polished. He always reminded Brooke of a bald and beardless Santa Claus except for the deep worry lines between his eyebrows.

"Is the boss here yet?" he asked Mrs. Forbes.

"No," answered Mrs. Gibson.

"I picked up an order that he ought to take a look at," said Sam.

"Do you want to wait, then?" asked Mrs. Forbes.

Sam checked his watch. "Yes, for a few minutes." He shook his head to her offer of coffee and moved out of Brooke's way.

"Now, where was I?" said Mrs. Gibson as if she'd been holding her breath. "Sam, you're just in time to hear my news. You won't believe this, but I have finally managed, after how many months, years would be more like it, to sell that house next door."

"That's wonderful, Dotty. Congratulations," said Mrs. Forbes.

"The old Harris place?" asked Sam.

Brooke stopped stacking clean plates. "I saw your FOR SALE sign was gone," she said.

"Oh, you did?" said Mrs. Gibson.

"Who bought it?" asked Brooke. "Do they have children?"

"Not they, dear. He. And most distinguished looking. Tall. A full head of white hair and never been married, I could swear to that."

"For heaven's sake, Dotty, how do you know?" asked Mrs. Forbes.

"One develops a sixth sense in my business, although —" Mrs. Gibson hesitated for an instant — "it is more difficult to tell with out-of-staters." She took another sip of coffee and a drag on her cigarette. It was amazing, thought Brooke. Mrs. Gibson was the only person Brooke knew who could drink and smoke and talk at the same time. "He called out of the blue yesterday," she was saying, "and arrived last night, late. Showing a house in the dark isn't easy, you know, but, as it turned out, the only thing he really wanted to see —" she paused for emphasis — "was the barn." The words came out on a billow of smoke.

"The barn! I know that barn!" exclaimed Sam. "It's infested with bats!"

"I warned him about them. And in the dead of night, can you imagine!" Smoke curled out of Mrs. Gibson's nose. She rolled on, "But he wouldn't listen. So, first I had to go home to get my flashlight, because I knew the electricity had been off in the barn since that storm last winter. And then, my dear, as soon as we opened the door and flashed the light around, that horde of bats, it seemed like hundreds of them, came swooping down from the rafters right at my head." Mrs. Gibson shuddered and sniffed. "And you know what they say about bats and hair."

"No. What?" asked Brooke.

"They're mad for it," answered Sam, "and once they're in it, it's the devil to get them out."

"Oh, Sam, really," said Mrs. Forbes.

"I know what I'm talking about, Marcie. It happened to me once when I was a kid. One of those blasted creatures came diving down from nowhere, right into my hair. My pop had to beat me over the head with a rake, and it wasn't the flexible kind either."

"Gosh, Sam, didn't that hurt?" asked Brooke. She tried not to stare at Sam's bald head. At least he's safe now, she thought.

"You bet it did, but it taught me something." Sam slammed a fist into the palm of his hand. "Kill 'em. Kill 'em first, ask questions later. Hell's wallpapered with them, my father always said."

"Well, *I* always say 'live and let live,' " said Mrs. Gibson. "Not that I like them, you understand. I felt like screaming, but my client did the weirdest thing. Just took the flashlight out of my hand and asked me to wait outside. And back in he went with all those creatures flying around!"

"Durn fool!" Sam shook his head. "In

the old days people knew how to get rid of vermin. We should have put a match to that barn long ago when we had the chance."

"I don't mind them outdoors," Mrs. Forbes said. "As long as they're not loose in the house."

"You'll never find one in my house," muttered Sam. "Not alive anyway."

"Well, there I was," Mrs. Gibson went right on, "in the pitch black, wondering what kind of person I was dealing with, when all of a sudden, out he came and closed the door as quiet as you please. Then he handed me the flashlight and said, 'I'll take it,' just like that. In all my born days I've never known anything so bizarre. And then this morning he showed up with a cashier's check for the full amount and the FOR SALE sign in the back of his car. He'd already taken it away. To save me the trouble, he said."

His house needs painting, thought Brooke suddenly. Wait 'til I tell Izzy. "When is he moving in?" she asked.

"Haven't a clue, dear. He's not the kind of person you ask." She leaned back in her chair and blew a long stream of smoke at the ceiling. "He's a doctor. Dr. Noah Blazer. It's always comforting, don't you think, to have a doctor right on your street."

"Health hazard, that's what they are.

Those bats." Sam was still shaking his head.

"He's not that kind of doctor. He's a PhD in one of the sciences," said Mrs. Forbes.

Brooke stared at her in surprise. Mom had known about him all along, she thought.

"Where did you hear that?" asked Mrs. Gibson.

"The druggist told me. When I was downtown. The grapevine is greased in this town." Brooke saw her mother frown and glance up at the ceiling as if she were waiting for a sound or something from Benji's room. Then the frown was gone, as quickly as it had come, and her mother's face was smooth and social again. But Brooke had the feeling that the frown was still there, just under the skin.

Chapter 3

The good smells in the kitchen made Brooke's stomach grumble. Her mother stirred gravy in the roasting pan on the top of the stove. Jason hung by his hands from the lintel of the kitchen door and hauled himself up and down. Over his grunting, Brooke heard an engine start and then the familiar clutch-bang of Sam's truck.

"Sam's left," she told her mother.

"*Now* can we eat?" asked Jason. He let himself drop. "That's seven chin-ups and Dad can only do ten."

"You've got sweat stains under your arms," said Brooke.

"Where's Benji?" asked Mrs. Forbes.

"Upstairs," said Brooke.

"Call him, would you, and light the candles. Jason, instead of picking at the hash browns, carry the platter in to the table."

The screen door slammed. "Dinner's on, Allen," called Mrs. Forbes.

"Be right there. I'll just wash my hands."

Mrs. Forbes served the food and passed the plates along. Mr. Forbes settled into his chair at the end of the table.

Super peas, thought Brooke. Fresh from the garden. Next to her Benji speared them one by one onto a tine of his fork and then slid the whole row into his mouth.

"Well," said Mr. Forbes, "it will be nice to see lights next door again."

"I'll say," agreed Brooke. "At night that empty house was like a dark hole. It made the street kind of eerie."

"Could be good for business, too," said her father. "Sam and I think I ought to drop by after Blazer moves in and have a chat with him."

"Now, wait a minute." Mrs. Forbes leaned to one side so she could see around the candlesticks. "What about the new shelves you've been promising me? My bindery is a shambles, and I've told you I've got a big commission arriving from Boston any day."

"What is it?" asked Brooke. "More hymnals?"

"No. Old law books. Two sets of a dozen volumes each. I understand they're all disbound — the front and back boards are off. Only the spines are intact. And Allen, there's no way I can restore so many without more work space. It would only take Sam a few days."

"The problem is, Sam doesn't have a few days," said Mr. Forbes. "This is our busiest season. I've got four houses to get framed in before the end of the summer and he's my right-hand man, not to mention the best carpenter I've got."

"Then have him work overtime. I'll pay for it," said Mrs. Forbes. "Listen, I get thirty-five dollars a book, at least . . . well, multiply it out yourself. We just can't ignore that kind of money."

"Eight hundred and forty dollars!" Brooke said.

"And that's the minimum," said her mother.

"Dad? What about soccer after supper?" asked Jason.

"You're interrupting," said Mrs. Forbes. "All I'm saying, Allen," she went on, "is put me on the top of the list before any new jobs."

"Delilah eats my lunches," said Benji suddenly.

"She what?" said his father.

"Eats my lunches," Benji repeated. "At least she used to." They were all looking at him.

"What lunches?" asked Brooke.

"My lunch bag lunches."

"You mean for school?" asked Brooke. Benji nodded. "Didn't you put them in your locker?"

"It happened before I got there," said Benji. "Sometimes. When you had to go early and I walked by myself."

"How could she?" Brooke asked him.

Benji cleared his throat. "Well, she sneaks up behind me and grabs it right out of my hand and eats it," he said. "She eats the paper bag, too. She did it twice last week. But she doesn't like fruit," he added.

"Good heavens!" said his mother. "Why didn't you tell me before school was out? No wonder you're so skinny. Have some more lamb and potatoes."

Maybe that's why he fainted, thought Brooke. From hunger.

Benji shook his head. "Can I be excused?" he asked. "There's something I want to do in my office."

"What about dessert? It's homemade pecan pie."

"I'd like an apple," said Benji. His mother leaned back and nodded. Benji knelt on his seat and reached across to the bowl of fruit. Then he climbed down and circled the table. As he passed behind her chair, Brooke felt him touch the back of her head twice, very gently.

"Can I have thirds?" asked Jason.

"That's disgusting," said Brooke. "Dad, do you think Dr. Blazer might want me and Izzy to paint? His sills are peeling."

"Could be," said her father. "Good thought."

The phone in the hallway rang.

"I'll get it." Mr. Forbes pushed back his chair.

The candles on each side of the fruit bowl flickered. The ringing stopped.

"Hello," she heard from the hall. "Oh, hello, Rosie. What can I do for you?"

Jason snorted. Brooke and her mother exchanged smiles.

"You hang on, Rosie, and I'll go get him." Brooke heard the clunk of the receiver and her father's footsteps on the stairs. Rosie Renwick, she thought. Pudgy little Rosie. Pudgy legs, pudgy fingers, pudgy braids. She'd been after Benji since the first day of school. It made Benji sigh, but he'd written her a couple of notes. Long ones, too.

"Uh, Rosie," her father was speaking again. "Are you still there? . . . Benji's busy right now. Is it important? Or can he call you in the morning?"

There was a pause. Jason played an imaginary violin.

"No. He's not sick. No. Not that I know of, I . . . What? . . . He did?" Brooke heard her father's voice turn sharp. His footsteps began to travel back and forth in the hall.

"Well, don't you worry any more about it, Rosie. Could have been anything. Probably it was something he ate for lunch. He's okay now. Perfectly okay. But thanks for calling. Right. Good-bye."

Brooke stole a glance down the table. Her mother's fork was halfway to her mouth but she was staring at her plate.

Her father came back into the dining room and sat down. He carefully respread his napkin over his knees.

"That was Rosie," he said. "She wanted to know how Benji was. She says he fell over in class."

Mrs. Forbes put down her fork. "He fainted, Allen. That's all. I was going to tell you, but you came home so late that I never had a chance."

"I assume you got to his teacher."

"It was too hectic when I picked him up and she had already left when I got back. So I decided to let it alone."

"The doctor says he has to take two pills now, instead of one," Brooke put in. "And he hates them."

"Dreadful dose," added Jason. His mouth was full of food.

Their father ignored them. "Call her," he said evenly.

"People have other things to think about over the summer, Allen."

"Call her anyway," said Mr. Forbes. It didn't sound like a suggestion. "I'll take care of Sam."

Their conversation was too closed and too careful, thought Brooke. They're fighting. She hugged her arms to her sides. The dining room suddenly seemed icy.

"I figured once you start explaining —" Mrs. Forbes began.

"Marcie, we'll discuss it later," Mr. Forbes interrupted. "Jason, don't lick your knife! You and Brooke can clear now."

"And bring in some ice cream with the pecan pie," added their mother.

Mr. and Mrs. Forbes went into the kitchen after supper and shut the door. Benji hadn't come down again, so Jason badgered Brooke into a one-on-one game of soccer on the front lawn. Even though it was barely dusk, he turned on the porch lights to make it seem more like a night game. Brooke defended her father's red pick-up truck, which Jason designated her goal, but after he scored four times she got bored. Back in the house she set up the triple tic-tac-toe game on the living room floor. There was no sound from the kitchen except the churning of the dishwasher. Izzy and I have a lot to do tomorrow, thought Brooke, rolling a marble between her fingers. Finish the fliers, get them

Xeroxed, but first we've got to decide whether we can raise our rates. We can say "experienced." Maybe we need a sign to put out in front when we're on a job so people know who's doing it. Like Mrs. Gibson does. "Painting by Forbes and Banuchi"? Or "Painting by Banuchi and Forbes"? That was alphabetical and sounded a little better, but it had been her idea.

The dishwasher stopped with a clunk.

". . . say anything, dammit. Flu." She heard her father's voice in the sudden silence. Loud and angry. "I won't have him singled out. People staring. . . ." The voice dropped to a low murmur. The dishwasher clicked and began to slosh again.

Someone came out of the kitchen. When Brooke looked up, her mother was standing in the doorway.

"Winning?"

Brooke nodded. One of her was winning on all three levels. Her mother still stood there.

"Listen, Brooke," she said after a moment, "about Benji's fainting. Let's keep it in the family. Shall we? No talking about it, okay? Not even with Izzy. Or Benji either, for that matter. Dad and I don't want to worry him unnecessarily."

"But suppose somebody asks me? What do I say?" asked Brooke.

"Say he's fine and leave it at that. It's

easier all the way around. Promise me? Okay?" Mrs. Forbes smiled.

Brooke felt a little jet of fear. Her mother sounded too positive and her smile was too stiff and went on too long. She looked down at the tic-tac-toe board.

"Okay. But just tell me why he has to take those huge pills."

"To keep him from doing it. To calm him down. He thinks too much. Maybe it's all that reading about animals and dinosaurs."

"Will the extra pill stop his fainting, then?" asked Brooke.

"Of course," said her mother.

Brooke couldn't look at her. For the first time in her life she felt her trust waver. She could feel her mother smiling down at her.

"Trust me," her mother said, turning away.

When Brooke headed upstairs a little while later, she noticed that the phone was gone from the hall table. The telephone cord led into the dining room and the dining room door was closed. For a moment she considered listening at the door and then decided against it. Someone might catch her at it.

The house was still and Brooke's room was dark except for a pale moonlight glow coming in through the thin curtains. She lay in bed trying to figure out what had awakened her. It couldn't have been a bad dream. There were no scary pictures left over in her mind. No unfinished homework. No tests. No school. There was no reason to be awake. She closed her eyes again and rolled over on her side, hollowing a soft place in her pillow with her cheek. It was then she heard it, a clack, clack, clack, a pause, then a whole series of clacks, a pause, then two more, like pebbles hitting a windowpane far away. She flopped over onto her back and frowned at the ceiling. Benji. The clacking began again in short bursts.

Brooke got out of bed and padded across the hooked rug into the bathroom they shared. The clacking was clearer there. She opened the far door quietly and peered into the darkness of his room.

The room was almost black because his shades were down, but a brilliant line of light rimmed the door to his box. The latch was swung back and she could make out the padlock hanging from the metal loop in the wood. A cord threaded out through a brightly lit notch at the base of the door and trailed off into the shadows along the wall.

At least he was in his office instead of prowling around the house, thought Brooke. She stood with her hand on the doorknob, debating whether or not to tell him to go back to bed. The clacking stopped. She could almost feel him thinking, scrunched over his typewriter in his pajamas, his chin in the palm of his hand. She wondered what the inside of his box looked like now. He hadn't let her see it for a long time, not since he'd shown her the old toy chest he had turned into a desk for the typewriter and she'd given him her wastebasket for a seat. He'd painted the wastebasket red.

He was typing again, quite fast and steadily. She wondered what he was writing. Whatever it was, it was long. If she closed both doors to the bathroom and put her pillow over her head, maybe she'd be able to block him out.

Back in her room she sat on the edge of her bed, testing. The clacks were so faint she had to strain to hear them. Her pillow would definitely do it. Brooke yawned and poked her legs back under the covers.

Then she heard something else, a snapping sound that repeated after a silence, and then two more snaps in quick succession, almost as irregular as the rhythm of Benji's typing. The sounds came from outside. Brooke was wide awake now. She tiptoed to the window and stared out, edging the curtain back with her hand. The first thing she saw was a lighted window in the house next door gleaming above the dark outline of the hedge of lilacs. He must have moved in already, she thought, without us knowing. The noise came again, sharp and clear, and something metallic flashed in the moonlight. She crouched down and leaned forward, ducking her head under the raised sash, until her nose touched the screen. It was then she saw the top of his head. Someone, it had to be Dr. Blazer, was moving along the far side of the lilac bushes clipping off the dead blooms one by one.

Chapter 4

Thursday afternoon smelled like rain. Wind rustled the tops of the maple trees, and the black and yellow undersides of the clouds looked bruised. Brooke got to the Green first and settled on the grass near the bandstand. It's going to pour, she thought.

"Hey, Brookie!" Izzy leaped a bench and came toward her at a gangling gallop, hitching at one of the straps of her painter's overalls. Her father's undershirt drooped at the neck and flapped under her arms, and her orange-red hair fizzled around her head.

"Done! Done in!" Izzy sank to her knees. "Dead!" She sprawled on her face and lay still. Brooke watched her back go up and down with each breath. Izzy lifted her head. "I plastered the town with them," she panted. "Even the Catholic church. I slid one under the door. The steeple's peeling."

"Steeple?" said Brooke. "Who's going to paint that? You faint if you're more than three inches off the ground."

"You can do it," said Izzy. "I'll hold the ladder." She mowed the grass around her with her fingers. "Which reminds me. Is Benji okay? I just heard he fainted in school."

"Where did you hear that?" asked Brooke.

"I don't know. Somebody? Mom?"

"He's fine," said Brooke quickly. "He was hungry or something. That's all. What did your father say about our great idea?"

Izzy's face cleared and she sat up. "Wait 'til you see it. You know Dad's paint-supply section? Well, I grabbed it all and jammed it into the window — brushes, ladders, rollers, mixers, everything. Then I piled a million paint cans in the middle and scotch-taped our notice to the top. It's a great display."

"Sounds like the town dump," said Brooke.

Izzy laughed. Her upper lip rolled back almost to her nose until all her top teeth and her gums showed. She sounded like a horse neighing and looked like a horse yawning. Brooke could never figure out how she did it.

"No, really," said Izzy. "It's terrific. My dad can't get over it. He's still out in the street staring at it. But I skipped the drugstore. I hate that 'el creepo' who runs it. He calls me 'doll.' "

Brooke wrinkled her nose and nodded. She looked the length of the Green. Across Maple Avenue she could see the new Cut-Rate Drugstore surrounded by a sea of black macadam. The brick facing of the store was so orange it seemed fake, and the paved parking lot was as big and flat as a soccer field. They had torn down the old inn and cut down most of the maple trees to build it. The parking lot was empty.

"Doesn't matter. No one ever goes there," she said.

"How'd you do?" asked Izzy. A blade of grass stuck to her bottom lip. "Got any left?"

"Nope. I only had one more after Dr. Blazer's so I stuck it in our mailbox."

"Dr. Blazer!" Izzy stared at Brooke. "You didn't!"

"I did. Why not?" Brooke looked puzzled. "We need a big job. And talk about peeling, I think he's got dry rot."

"You're the one with dry rot — of the brain!" Izzy exploded. "The man's totally weird!"

"Oh, come off it, Izzy," said Brooke. "Stop exaggerating. It's just that he's new.

Maybe we seem weird to him. Just look over there for starters." She motioned with a jerk of her head. On the other side of Main Street a group of boys from Jason's class sat on the cannon in front of the post office. Ricky Renwick straddled the barrel, bent forward, stuffing something that looked like a Coke bottle down the muzzle. Other kids lounged against the pyramid of cannon balls, waiting for a turn to get on, or tussled and wrangled between the petunia beds. From now on, all summer long, there would be kids on or around the cannon. Always, the same ones, thought Brooke. They waved at passing cars and yelled things that made them hoot with laughter. Big deal.

"Oh, gross out," moaned Izzy. "Fat Ricky. Revolting!"

"They're all revolting. He's no worse than the rest."

"True. I guess he's just normal revolting." Izzy turned back to Brooke. "But I still say Dr. Blazer is positively abnormal weird. You said so yourself when you told me about him chopping down the lilac bushes. And remember what happened when your mom and dad tried to be friendly?"

"Nothing."

"Exactly. He's never come over for coffee. And he's never invited them in."

"But, Izzy, he only moved in last week."

Izzy ignored her. "And you don't even know what happened this morning."

"What do you mean, this morning?" asked Brooke.

"I mean, just listen to this." Izzy's voice dropped to a whisper. "When Dad and I opened up, he was already there. Waiting by the door. He looked as if he'd camped there all night."

"All night?"

"Well," Izzy replied, "he was there before we were, and Dad opens practically at dawn during the summer. And then, almost before my father had a chance to turn on the lights, he'd bought out half the store. Hammers, nails, hooks, tons of window shades, the blackout kind, and the best, most expensive flashlight. I think it even works underwater. It's as big as a searchlight." Izzy indicated an enormous circle with her hands in front of Brooke's face. "And what he didn't buy, he ordered!"

"So," said Brooke. "It's good for business."

"You haven't heard what he ordered. Get this." Izzy took a breath. "Two hundred and fifty yards of wire, piano wire," Izzy said, looking intently at Brooke, "and thirty dozen bells." She paused between each word. "And on top of that, he tried to order one eyedropper. My father sent him to the drugstore for that." Izzy leaned back on her straightened arms.

"Bells? What kind of bells?" Brooke asked.

"Those dinky metal ones that you put on Christmas packages or around cats' necks. And it's June and he doesn't have a cat or a dog or anything. Mrs. Gibson said so."

Brooke was multiplying and adding in her head. Thirty dozen. Three hundred and sixty bells. She tried to picture them piled up or in a basket or spread out on the floor, but she couldn't. There were too many of them. They kept lurching and skittering out of her mind.

"And you know, don't you, what they use piano wire for?" Izzy hunched closer to Brooke until their knees touched. "To strangle people!"

"Oh, Izzy, pianos, too," said Brooke. "But okay, if it makes you so nervous, we'll just go get it out of his mailbox."

She stood up and started off across the Green. Izzy followed.

"What if he's already picked up his mail?" she asked.

They jogged down Walden Street. Izzy jumped an imaginary hurdle.

"What if he's read it?" she went on.

Brooke kicked a stone into the street. She wished Izzy would shut up.

"He's probably called us already," said

Izzy. "And your mother's said yes. We'll be forced to paint, and then one day, late in the afternoon, when it's getting dark and we're helpless on the ladders, he'll sneak up behind us with a piece of that wire. . . ."

They turned into Ashpotag Road. Brooke checked her driveway. "I forgot," she said. "It's Jason's first day at soccer camp. Mom isn't even home."

"Dr. Blazer is," said Izzy. The rear of a khaki-colored van stuck out beyond the end of the lilac hedge.

Dark clouds piled into the sky. For an instant a stray shaft of sunlight blinded Dr. Blazer's windows. Brooke looked across his driveway to the mailbox. It was nailed to a wooden post at the edge of the road.

"Somebody's been there. I put the flag up and now it's down," she said. "I'll check."

"How?" Izzy grabbed hold of the back of Brooke's shirt. "You can't just march out there. There isn't a shred of cover. That mailbox sticks up like a scarecrow. He'll think we're stealing." A gust of wind turned the leaves of the lilacs silver-side up. "And it's about to pour rain," she finished with a groan.

Brooke felt Izzy's fingers twisting her shirt. She's working herself into a stew, she thought, but on the other hand, going into someone else's mailbox was probably a federal offense. "Wait here," she ordered, pulling away. "I'll be right back."

She found Izzy crouching under the lilacs when she returned.

"Someone's been howling and howling," Izzy whispered. "I think it's coming from his cellar."

Brooke listened. "That's just Delilah. She's scared of thunderstorms." She opened a large brown-and-white umbrella. It blossomed over her head like a parachute.

"What's that for? It's not raining yet," said Izzy.

"Get under anyway. We're going for a walk."

"Why? Where? Oh, brilliant. Terrific! Do you think it will work?"

"I'll hold it low," said Brooke, "so it covers both our heads. But you walk in the road. You're taller. Ready? Start on the left foot. One, two, three, go!"

The umbrella came down past Brooke's shoulder. All she could see was a strip of pavement and grass and Izzy's feet. Izzy snorted and wheezed. "Who would believe an umbrella with legs," she said.

"He'll never recognize us from the waist down," said Brooke. The bottom of the mailbox post came into view. "Stop giggling. It's dead ahead and —"

"Don't mention dead," pleaded Izzy.

"Shut up and listen. When we get there we stop, as if we were talking or something. Then I'll tilt the umbrella and screen us and the mailbox from the house. You open the box and whip out our ad, fast. Fast as you can. Okay? Now!"

"Oh, jeez, it's too stiff!" grunted Izzy. "Oh, sugar! It's too stuffed. Letters. Newspapers. I'll have to take everything out. Oh, shoot!"

The mail papered the ground like playing cards. Izzy dropped to all fours. Brooke and the umbrella followed her down.

"Oh, help! It's all over the road," said Izzy. "It's getting grubby."

The umbrella spokes rested on the sidewalk. Brooke reached for a sheet of paper.

"I've found it. Our thing." She crumpled it up and stuffed it into her pocket.

"Hey. There are no stamps on half this stuff," said Izzy, inspecting an envelope. "And he used to live at the Subsurface Research Institute. It's all been forwarded. Here's one from someplace called the Air Force Avionics Laboratory. And ever heard of the Aberdeen Proving Grounds?"

"Cut it out, Izzy! We've got what we came for. Put those back. Here. These, too."

"All right. All right," said Izzy. "There. Flag up or down?"

"Down." Brooke swung around and

grabbed the umbrella with her other hand. "Let's get out of here," she said. "Not so fast. Don't run." But when they were past the hedge of lilacs, Izzy broke for Brooke's front porch.

"Safe," she gasped when they were both under the roof. "Nobody saw us."

Thunder cracked in the distance and the first spatters of rain blotched the steps. Brooke furled the umbrella and produced the creased paper from her pocket.

"Here's our ad," she said and smoothed it out. FORBES & BANUCHI was emblazoned across the top in bold, black, hand-lettering.

Izzy didn't even look at it. She slid her back down the clapboard wall of the house until she was sitting on the porch floor. "What's an avionics laboratory anyway?" she asked.

"Don't know," said Brooke. Probably had something to do with airplanes, she thought, or maybe explosives. One of the letters she'd seen had come from The National Bomb Data Center.

"I told you he was strange," said Izzy. "He's probably a mad scientist."

What did it matter, thought Brooke. They had retrieved the ad. They wouldn't have to deal with him.

The steps glistened with water and rain roared on the roof. The sight of water dripping from the eaves made her thirsty, and the telephone was ringing. Brooke went to answer it.

"It was the riding stable," she announced gleefully when she hung up. "Our first job. They want us to paint the standards and cavallettis again."

Chapter 5

It rained for two days; and then it stopped, leaving a scrubbed blue sky. The clouds seemed to have been washed away forever. Morning after morning dawned bright and hot, and every evening the sun set in a blaze of red. Brooke was glad for the sun during the first week that she and Izzy worked at the stables, but after a while it was like a friend who came for an overnight and stayed too long. Brooke's arms turned dark brown up to the sleeves of her tee shirt and Izzy's nose burnt red and peeled. Mr. Forbes gave them a couple of old painters' caps, and Brooke tied her hair in a ponytail to keep it off her neck, but still the sun beat down on their heads and backs. By the time they finished the stable job a few wells had run dry. Mr. Banuchi explained that the water table was already low because there hadn't been much snow over the winter, and Mrs. Gibson reported that people had begun to bring their laundry to town. There was a waiting line for the machines next to the drugstore.

In the garden the earth cracked. The lettuce wilted and the tops of the onions drooped. The Fourth of July came and went and the corn remained knee high.

One evening after the sun had gone down, Brooke attached an extension to the hose, and she and her mother took turns watering with one hand and slapping at mosquitoes with the other. Afterward they went into Mrs. Forbes's bindery and daubed calamine lotion on the red welts. The law books from the private collector had arrived and were still in their opened boxes on the floor.

"Izzy and I will paint the shelves for you," offered Brooke, "for half price."

"If Sam ever builds them," her mother said. Later Brooke heard her in the living room. "Allen, I mean it this time. If you don't get Sam Renwick in here soon, I'm going to pile those books on your side of the bed."

"I'm doing my best," Brooke heard her father answer.

"Meanwhile the books are on the floor," her mother reminded him.

And Izzy and I are out of work, thought Brooke. If we were carpenters we'd be golden. Maybe I ought to take shop next year.

Bored, she went to find Benji. He was in his room at his worktable, and he looked so startled to see her that she felt a pang of guilt. She'd been ignoring him. She had no idea what he'd been up to.

"What are you doing?" she asked.

Benji hunched over his table, shielding something with his shoulder and arm.

"Nothing. Making more dinosaurs for my collection."

His shades were partway down and his face was in shadow.

"Want to come with me to get a creamy? I'll treat you."

Benji thought for a moment. "Are all those kids on the cannon?" he asked finally.

"Where else?"

"I'm not that hungry."

"What about a bike ride?"

"I think my tires are flat," said Benji.

"Maybe you can still ride on my handlebars."

"I'm too busy," said Benji. "Working."

"Which dinosaurs are you making?" asked Brooke.

Benji hesitated. Then he cleared his throat. "A stegosaur and an ankylosaur."

"Can I see?"

"No. They're not done yet." He turned

his head away. "If Mom's going downtown, you could ask her to get me more clay."

Brooke wandered off. A creamy would just make me fat, she decided, but I could get him the clay myself. There was nothing else to do anyway.

But the next afternoon the Pritchards came through. Their deck needed scrubbing and two coats of Cuprinol. It wasn't the greatest job in the world, but Brooke and Izzy didn't have any other offers and the Pritchards paid by the hour. "We can stretch it, a little," said Izzy.

As it turned out, the job stretched itself. The pale green mold that stained the boards and railing had to be scoured off with wire brushes and buckets of Clorox and water. Late in the afternoon of the third day, Brooke's shoulders began to ache, and sweat ran down the sides of Izzy's face and dripped off the end of her chin. Brooke put down her brush and lifted her wet hair off the back of her neck. Her hands smelled of Clorox.

"I wonder," said Izzy, "if we got this job because the Pritchards saw our ad, or because Dad stripped his flower beds for their daughter's wedding last summer. If it was Dad, remind me to tell him to keep his flowers to himself."

"We're almost done with the bad part,"

said Brooke. "The Cuprinol is easy. We can just slosh it on."

"Is your mom picking us up again?" asked Izzy.

"Yes. On her way back from soccer camp."

"Think I'll go and wash up." Izzy opened the sliding screen doors. "Remember, you're coming to my house for supper." The latch on the door clicked shut behind her.

Brooke dumped the leftover Clorox solution under the deck and stowed the brushes and pails in a corner. A horn beeped in the driveway.

"Where's Izzy?" asked Mrs. Forbes when Brooke reached the station wagon.

"Coming," said Brooke. She went around to the other side but put off getting in. Benji sat in front, but Jason and his friends had folded down the second seat and were sprawled all over the back.

Izzy banged out of the house and tore across the gravel. The hair on top of her head was wet and parted in the middle. Oh, no, she's done the bobby pin bit, thought Brooke. Rows of bobby pins plastered Izzy's hair to her head down to her ears. Izzy was trying to teach her hair a lesson. But it wouldn't learn. Already it was beginning to frizz again.

Brooke got into the car first and took Benji on her lap. The top of his head still fit under her chin but it wouldn't for much longer, she thought with a pang. He felt light and cool, and his arms, resting on hers, looked strangely white against her tan.

"You smell like laundry," he said.

The rest of the car smelled of sweat and damp socks and feet. Jason faced the rear window, his back against the front seat right behind Brooke. She could see a piece of him in the rearview mirror. He was juggling his soccer ball and letting it bounce on the floor of the car, casually. Every now and then he rolled his head as if he were trying to work out a cramp. His army jacket was knotted around his neck, even though Brooke figured it must be ninety degrees or more.

She tightened her arms around Benji and looked away from the mirror, but she could still hear the irregular thump, thump of the ball and the endless boring soccer talk. Squat thrusts, push-ups, super saves, and dribbles. Apparently, it had been a tough workout. Everyone complained about how flaked they were, except for Jason. For Jason it had been a snap, as usual. He'd done everything longer or faster or better. He'd run more laps than anyone.

"Anyone ever," said Jud Hall. "Four more than me."

"Pain," said Jason. "A lot of pain."

At the beginning of camp Jason had been issued the number-ten jersey. Pele's number. Hank Rosen said for the fiftieth time that he thought that might mean something. The coach had put a hand on Jason's shoulder during practice again. Jud thought that might mean something, too.

"You're getting pretty good yourself, Jud," said Jason. "On my last goal. Remember the one you almost blocked? That was some dive you made!"

"Jason's so obvious," Brooke whispered to Izzy. "He spreads the praise around just so he can end up wiping the knife on himself."

"Disgusting," agreed Izzy, but Brooke noticed that she kept eyeing the back of Jason's head.

Mr. Banuchi was watering his flower beds when they got to Izzy's house. As soon as he saw the car he turned off the hose and produced a pair of heavy-duty scissors.

"Wait two minutes, Marcie," he called to Mrs. Forbes, "and I'll have some daisies and snapdragons for you."

Brooke and Izzy got out of the car. Mr. Banuchi bent over his flowers, picking and choosing, criticizing and praising. A prize beckoned just beyond his reach. He leaned toward it, balancing precariously on one foot, trying not to fall into the pansies and alyssum.

"You can say hello later," Izzy told Brooke. "This could take hours."

Mrs. Banuchi was having a beer at the kitchen sink. She was large and chunky with short graying hair and Brooke always thought she looked more like a grandmother than a mother, before she remembered that she was both. And Izzy was an aunt. All of her brothers were grown up and two had wives and little kids of their own. Izzy's other brother, Mike, worked with Izzy's father in the hardware store.

That night Mike was late getting home. Mrs. Banuchi waited supper.

"Just as I was closing, Dr. Blazer came to pick up his order," Mike explained, pulling something out of his pocket. "He paid with this."

It was a one-hundred-dollar bill, crisp and unwrinkled. Brooke had never seen one before. Mrs. Banuchi rubbed her fingers over it and held it up to the light.

"Counterfeit?" asked Izzy hopefully.

"Real," Mrs. Banuchi said. "I'll enter it in the books in the morning."

"Government money," said Mr. Banuchi. "Too big for this town."

Mrs. Banuchi folded the bill in half and

tucked it down the front of her dress. Brooke wished she'd had a chance to see whose picture was on it.

"Have a few bobby pins," Mike said to Izzy. "And who's your cute friend? Don't tell me. Let me guess. I've seen that face somewhere before. The new drugstore!" He snapped his fingers and grinned at Brooke. "That's it. Your picture's pinned up on the cash register. Right next to Izzy's."

"It is?" said Brooke. She never knew whether to believe him or not.

"Yeah. A before-and-after for hair straightener. You're the after."

"Oh, shut up," said Izzy.

Mike jabbed at her chin and ruffled the front of her head, messing up the line of bobby pins. "Had you going for a minute, didn't I, frizz?" he said.

"What are you gabbing about?" asked Mrs. Banuchi.

"Private joke," Mike told her.

"Older brothers are better," Brooke said to Izzy later that evening.

"What's wrong with Benji? He's okay," said Izzy. "Isn't he?"

"I wasn't talking about Benji," said Brooke quickly.

"I think Jason's funny," said Izzy.

"Conceited, you mean."

Izzy didn't answer for a moment. She

was making faces at herself in the mirror, sucking in her cheeks to make her cheekbones show and widening her eyes. "Brooke, have you . . . I mean . . . promise you won't laugh if I ask you something."

"Yeah. What?"

"Have you ever kissed anyone?" Izzy blurted out. "I mean a boy or something?"

"No," Brooke said. "Not really."

"I guess our development's retarded," said Izzy. She sounded relieved.

The whole thing's disgusting, thought Brooke. It's time to go home, anyway.

"Are you sure you'll be all right?" Mr. Banuchi wanted to know when Brooke went to say good night.

"Positive," said Brooke. She waved to Izzy in the lighted doorway.

The moon was a sliver and there were no streetlights, but Brooke had walked that way too often to count. Every dark shape was a familiar tree or bush or house. Only the details were missing and the colors exchanged for shades of gray.

Izzy was lucky, thought Brooke, being the youngest. Nobody breathing down her neck. And nobody to worry about. Like Benji. Izzy baby-sat sometimes for her brothers' kids, but that wasn't the same. When the parents came back, Izzy could go home and forget about them. It was different with her and Benji. She'd taken care of him almost every afternoon when he was a baby. She knew everything about him. Almost everything.

In the distance Brooke heard someone whistling and calling. It sounded like Mrs. Gibson. Brooke had stopped to listen, when something large and alive slammed into her from the side. She staggered back and was trying to regain her balance when she was rushed at again.

"Oh, Delilah, you idiot dog! Get off me!" Delilah slathered and sluffered at her face. Brooke shoved the paws off her shoulders. "Down!" Delilah nosed her hands and snuffled at her bluejeans. "Stop it, dimwit!"

Delilah bounded about in front of Brooke and ambushed her ankles. Brooke was forced to kick out at her. Delilah loved it and came back for more. Brooke fended her off until they reached the corner opposite Mrs. Gibson's house. The calling was loud and clear now.

"Go home, pea brain," said Brooke.

Headlights blazed up behind her. Delilah abandoned the game and crouched, flat and panting, in the shadows by the side of the road. As the car passed she sprang out and took off after it. Brooke watched the red taillights diminish to pinpricks and then disappear.

"Din-din, Delilah," called Mrs. Gibson.

Brooke heard the repeated slamming of

a car door. "Car-car, Delilah," Mrs. Gibson yodeled. She was down to her last resort. Delilah loved to go for drives. Sometimes the door trick worked. Brooke headed down Ashpotag Road without waiting to find out.

She could see the outline of Dr. Blazer's house and the dull, metallic gleam of his mailbox. The dark bulk of his van was parked in his driveway. Brooke stayed on the far side of the road until she was well past the lilac hedge.

The night was warm and windless. There were lights on in the kitchen at home but the porch light was off. Brooke cut across the lawn and went up the steps.

Something creaked in the stillness. The black curve of the hammock strung across the corner of the porch shifted slightly.

"Jason?"

"No. It's me."

"Benji? What are you doing out here? Aren't you supposed to be in bed?"

"Shh. Mom will hear you." The hammock jiggled. "Look."

Brooke walked the length of the porch. There was a glimmer in the middle of the hammock.

"What have you got?"

"Fireflies," said Benji, "in a jar." He held it up for her to see. Lights flickered between the dark silhouettes of his fingers.

"How did you catch so many? Must be dozens in there."

"About a hundred."

"Move over," said Brooke.

Benji sat up, holding the jar in both hands, and swung his legs over the side of the hammock. His bare feet dangled above the porch floor. The hammock sagged under Brooke's weight. She pushed to start it swinging. They swayed in silence, listening to the trill of the crickets beyond the porch railing and staring at the jar.

"Look, Benj," said Brooke after a while. "They seem to be lighting up in a kind of rhythm."

"I know. Like ships signaling at night. But I don't know why they do it. Nobody does for sure. Sometimes thousands of them get together and light up at exactly the same moment, as if someone plugged them in. Like a Christmas tree."

"You're making that up."

"No, I'm not. It happens in Malaysia," said Benji. "And you know what else? They can save people's lives. In Cuba once, a surgeon did an emergency operation with only fireflies for light."

Brooke looked down. The light from the jar barely illuminated Benji's knees. "How could he see what to take out and what to leave in?"

"He could see enough," said Benji. "In South America the fireflies are much bigger. Three of them could light up this whole jar. They're as bright as flames. Ladies even wear them around their necks and in their hair instead of diamonds."

"You couldn't pay me to put bugs in my hair," said Brooke. "That's worse than bats."

Benji shifted in the hammock. "I like bats," he said. Inside the jar, sparks of light flared and died out and flared again.

"I might get a job as firefly catcher," he went on. "I could sell them, you know, for a lot of money. Premium prices. Maybe a penny a bug."

"Who'd buy them?" asked Brooke.

"Scientists," answered Benji. "Because firefly light isn't hot like a light bulb. It's cold. And scientists want to know how to make it. But they need luciferin and luciferase. And oxygen, of course. But everybody has that. So they have to keep buying fireflies."

"Lucifer . . . what?"

"Luciferin and luciferase." Benji cleared his throat. "Those are the chemicals in a firefly that make it light up," he went on patiently. "And scientists haven't figured out how to reproduce the stuff yet. Actually, I don't think anyone's figured out anything much about fireflies, except that they're a mystery." Benji lifted the jar and held it in front of his face. "Like me," he added.

The hammock stopped abruptly. Brooke turned her head to look at her brother, but Benji seemed to have forgotten what he'd said. He'd raised the jar higher and was squinting at the fireflies through the glass bottom, his mouth open.

"Have you been taking your pills?" she asked him.

Somebody turned on a light in the living room. The windows nearest them shone yellow.

"Benji? Benji Forbes! Where are you?"

Benji lowered the jar. "Uh oh, it's Mom," he said. He wriggled out of the hammock and ducked under the cord that attached it to the side of the house.

"Good idea," said Brooke. "Zap up the back stairs. I'll cover for you."

Benji cradled the jar in his arms. "You know what? I wish I could be a firefly," he whispered, "for the summer."

Mrs. Forbes opened the screen door and came out onto the porch. But Benji was gone.

Chapter 6

Brooke was having a dream. She knew it was a dream but she couldn't wake herself out of it. She and Izzy with Benji in the middle were sitting on a wide wooden swing suspended from chains. The Banuchis' swing, but not the Banuchis' backyard. The Pritchards' yard. The three of them pumped in unison, laughing, to get the swing moving, but then it seemed to soar by itself higher and higher into the sky. When it swooped back, they were hundreds of feet above the ground. Brooke clung to the chain on one side and put her other arm around Benji to keep him from falling. He was slipping away from her. She held him so tightly it hurt.

Suddenly Benji was gone. The swing arced closer and closer to the sun. The heat pressed down on Brooke's head and blistered her face. The sides of her throat stuck together. She tried to swallow. She tried to stop the swing. She couldn't hang on any longer.

Brooke woke up in a tangle of sheets. Her pillow was flattened and her shoulders ached. She kicked free of the covers and sat up, still groggy with dream and sleep. For a while she sat without moving, staring at the foot of her bed and feeling the ache draped like a heavy towel across her neck and down her arms. Either she'd slept wrong or it was all that scrubbing with the Clorox.

There was no cool side to the pillow, and the bottom sheet had come untucked. The mattress ticking showed. Brooke tried shifting over and pulling at a corner of the sheet to straighten it, but it didn't work. The bed was a mess of ridges and wrinkles. She'd have to get up and remake the whole thing. But first she wanted something to drink.

She was thinking cold water, lots of it, when a pinprick of light gleamed in the darkness next to her bureau. The light disappeared. Then there was another flash closer to the floor and another in the corner by her rocking chair. Fireflies. Benji's. They must have escaped. Her room was infested with them.

Brooke got out of bed. Both bathroom doors were open. Fireflies winked above Benji's bed and near his box and by his worktable. But Benji wasn't there. The bed was empty and the box was locked, but the shade on his front window was raised. The window was open and the screen had been propped outward with a ruler. On the windowsill was the firefly jar. The top of the jar was on the sill next to it. He must have tried to let them go.

Brooke checked the room again, even the crack between the bed and the wall, just in case. Gone on one of his night rambles, she decided. Downstairs, probably, to the living room. He liked the changed look of the chairs and sofas in the dark. Or to the kitchen for some fruit. Fruit made her think orange juice and ice cubes.

She went out through the door of his room and tiptoed along the hall and down the stairs, feeling for each step. It was dark at the bottom, but the deserted kitchen with its white appliances seemed bathed in fish light.

Brooke opened the door of the icebox and squinted into the bright interior. A glass pitcher of orange juice stood next to the cartons of milk. Brooke couldn't wait. She picked it up with both hands and drank directly from the spout. Then she wiped her chin on her arm and licked the drips off the side of the pitcher. There was only a film of juice left at the bottom, but she put the pitcher back in the icebox anyway and closed the door.

"Benji?" she called softly into the living room. "Benji?" No answer.

He didn't usually go outside, but maybe he was in the hammock. She opened the front doors and went out onto the porch. The hammock was slack, but on the railing near the steps she found a small apple core. It had been eaten to within an inch of its life. Benji had been there and gone.

Where was he, then? It was cooler outside. Brooke sat down on the top step, her arms wrapped around her knees, wondering if something had happened to him. Nothing moved on the road and the house behind her was quiet, but the night was full of noises, chirpings and croakings and the rustle and creep of the ground breathing and water seeping and the business of animals. Pale wisps of fog hovered above the grass. He's out there somewhere, Brooke thought, but where? A black shape swooped out of the darkness and skimmed past her, so close that she ducked. Too close for a bird. A bat. The step and the air seemed to grow colder, and her nightgown, where it touched her, felt clammy. She shivered and yawned.

There was a sound from the driveway. And then another. The gravel crunched. Brooke turned her head.

Above the roof of the porch the sky was aglow. Brooke hadn't noticed it before. For a moment she thought it might be northern lights, but it was too low and not far enough away. She hesitated and then got up and walked slowly across the wet grass, sticking close to the porch wall and pausing every few steps to look back over her shoulder. The night seemed to lift as she neared the driveway. Still, when she turned the corner of the house, the blaze of light beyond the lilac hedge confused her. Instinctively she reached out a hand and touched the wood of the porch.

The light was coming from Dr. Blazer's barn. It was all lit up, as if he were giving a party. In the middle of the night. A silent party. With no guests. A party for himself.

And Benji, Brooke thought suddenly. Benji, too, I'll bet. Bet he saw the light and was curious. Benji was over there in the barn with him. She knew it.

He shouldn't be there. They didn't know Dr. Blazer. One of Brooke's knees was trembling. Someone had to go get him. She pushed off from the house and crept across the driveway, feeling unprotected and alone in her thin nightgown and wishing she'd put on her bathrobe or sweatshirt or something. When she reached the hedge, she crouched down and peered between the leaves. The doors of the barn were wide open. Light flooded out toward the road.

Someone moved across the opening. Tall, in a khaki jacket like Jason's. Dr. Blazer. His white hair gleamed in the light and then the edge of the doorway cut him off. Brooke waited, but there was no sign of Benji. Where was he? What was Dr. Blazer doing with him? How could she get him out of there?

There were two windows in the near side of the barn. On her hands and knees Brooke began to work her way along the hedge toward them. The hem of her nightgown caught and tugged and then the light went out.

Brooke stood up, listening, her eyes wide. For a moment she felt blinded and deaf. Then she heard the creak and scrape of doors and the click of metal on metal. Was Dr. Blazer locking him up? It was impossible, but where else could he be? Then she became aware of the intermittent murmur of voices.

"Night, Noah." Benji's voice was so close it startled her. Brooke stepped back, hugging her chest. She heard footsteps going away.

A twig snapped and a small white figure materialized out of the lilacs and trotted toward the house. Brooke felt shaky with relief.

"Benji! Stop! Where on earth have you been?"

Benji pulled up short and turned around. "Oh, hi, Brooke."

"What are you doing out here? I've been looking all over for you and I'm freezing," whispered Brooke. The pebbles on the driveway cut into her bare feet. "You just can't go wandering off in the middle of the night."

"I didn't think you'd wake up. You were sound asleep. I heard you snoring."

"I don't snore," hissed Brooke. "And, darn it, Benji, you shouldn't sneak off like that."

His face looked pale and defenseless in the darkness. Suddenly Brooke was tired of anger and worry. "I'm hungry," she said. "Are you?"

Benji nodded.

"Want to raid the icebox?"

"Sure." Benji set off again and Brooke followed him into the house. This time she turned on the light in the kitchen.

"Your sneakers are sopping," she said. Benji looked down. His laces draggled. "Take them off." Benji perched obediently on a kitchen chair. He tugged at his sneakers and dropped them on the floor.

"There's grass stuck to your feet," he said. "And your nightgown's all dirty."

"What do you want to eat? Apple wedges and honey?" asked Brooke.

"And hot buttered toast with sugar," he added. "I can make that."

"Okay, but keep it quiet."

"There's an empty juice pitcher in here," said Benji a moment later.

"Forget it. Bring milk instead."

They assembled everything on the table. Brooke set two glasses and the bowl of sugar between them. Benji had already dipped a section of apple into the jar of honey and was waiting for it to finish dripping. Brooke watched the thin gold thread spiral onto his plate. She wondered whether he had slept at all.

"What were you doing at Dr. Blazer's?" she asked finally. "You shouldn't go over there, you know."

"Why not?" Benji gnawed on the piece of apple, protecting his loose tooth.

"You just shouldn't. There are things you don't know about him. He's strange."

Benji ate the crust off one side of his piece of toast. Then he cleared his throat and looked up at her. "There are things I don't know about me," he said. "I'm strange, too."

"You are not!" Brooke was so surprised she almost shouted.

"Yes, I am," said Benji. There were

shadows under his eyes. "You remember that last day at school? When Mom had to come and get me? I woke up on the floor by my desk. At first I didn't know where I was and then I saw all the other kids staring down at me. They looked scared to death — as if I were a monster or dead or something. And when I was waiting in the nurse's room they made crazy faces at me through the window."

"They're dumb, that's why!" said Brooke fiercely.

Benji reached for the sugar bowl. "But I don't care about them," he said. "Noah likes me."

Brooke felt a tightness in her chest as if she'd held her breath too long. She picked up a piece of apple, but she wasn't hungry. Benji had never mentioned his fainting before. She wondered whether he remembered that she'd been there that time in the bathroom and if he was asking her to tell him about it. Maybe he wasn't. Not really. She sneaked a look at him, but his head was bent and he was sprinkling sugar on his toast. Maybe she ought to talk to him anyway, no matter what Mom said. But what could she tell him? What did she know? Brooke stared into her glass of milk.

"Noah's like me, I think," he said. "In some ways. He's a night owl. No, not an owl. Owls are stupid. A night pigeon." He smiled, looking pleased with himself. "Pigeons are smart. Much smarter than people think."

"What are you talking about? Homing pigeons? The ones that carry messages?"

"And other kinds, too. Photo-reconnaissance pigeons and detection pigeons and missile-guidance pigeons...." Benji paused and looked at Brooke's face. "You don't believe me, do you?" He sounded happy. "But it's true. In the Second World War, radar wasn't as good. It could only direct missiles from ground to air. So they trained pigeons to guide the missiles the other way."

"Pigeons?" When Benji got interested in something he soaked it up like a paper towel. "Pigeons?" she repeated.

"Pigeons," said Benji, his head nodding. "They never got a chance to do it, but they were ready. They could have done it. It would have worked. Noah said so. And they're still being trained right now. Not for missiles. For detection. To search and report, just like Indian scouts."

"Report what?"

"Military targets, troop movements, even ambushes," answered Benji. "The army was thinking of using them in the Vietnam War against the guerillas. The pigeons would fly ahead carrying this tiny electronic pack and signal back if there were men hiding in the bushes."

"But don't they camouflage themselves to look like bushes? A pigeon can't tell the difference," Brooke insisted.

Benji picked up another piece of apple. "Pigeons can tell, all right, even if the man sticks branches and leaves in his helmet."

Brooke had never thought much about pigeons before. Benji washed the apple down with the last of his milk. "They can discriminate," he said. "Ordinary old pigeons."

"Where did you learn all this stuff?"

Benji yawned. "I'll ask Noah if you can come to our experiment," he said.

"What experiment?" asked Brooke sharply. "Is he experimenting on you?"

"We're doing it together."

"No, you're not. And don't go back there again," said Brooke. "And you shouldn't call him by his first name, either."

Benji didn't answer.

Brooke remembered something else. "That barn is full of bats. I'll tell Mom. I mean it, Benj."

Benji yawned and checked his loose tooth with a finger. His head nodded to the side. He's either wide awake or sound asleep, thought Brooke. No in-between.

"Hey!" she said. "Come on. Don't sleep here. Help clean up."

When Brooke reached her room, there was only one firefly left, but it had stopped sparking. Now it was just a bug on her pillow. She went to tell Benji about them.

Benji was on his bed but not in it. He was hanging upside down by his knees from his headboard. The top of his pajamas was bunched around his armpits and she could see the hollow of his stomach and his belly button above the arch of his ribs. His head rested on his pillow and his eyes were closed. Brooke forgot about the fireflies.

"Are you all right?" she asked.

"I'm sleeping."

"Upside down?"

Benji smiled without opening his eyes. Upside down his smile looked funny. Too many teeth. "I'm trying to find out what it feels like," he said.

Chapter 7

The next morning Brooke overslept. Her mother had left to drive Jason to soccer camp but there was a note on the kitchen table.

"Good Morning! Who put the empty O.J. pitcher back in the icebox?? Love, Mom." Mrs. Forbes had drawn a smily face.

The sun was already hot and hard on the road. Brooke ran past Dr. Blazer's house, still tucking her shirt into her bluejean cut-offs. All the new shades on Dr. Blazer's windows were pulled down. She thought of telling Izzy about him and Benji but decided against it. Izzy would just go off into one of her ghoulish fits.

The cuprinoling at the Pritchards' was finished by late afternoon, and Izzy invited Brooke to spend the night to celebrate. The next morning at breakfast, Mr. Banuchi asked them if they were free to paint storm windows.

"Stacked in the garage," he said. "Paint, too."

Izzy eye-checked with Brooke. "Okay. Sure. But our usual rates," she said. "No family discount."

Mr. Banuchi grunted. "Blasted drought. The soil is as hard as brick," he said to Mrs. Banuchi.

"Good, dear," said Mrs. Banuchi from behind her newspaper. She blew into her coffee.

When Brooke got home after lunch, not only was Benji's door shut, but there was also a black-crayoned *Do Not Disturb* sign hanging from his doorknob. She stood looking at the sign for a long time, wondering what was going on in there, wondering if he'd been holed up in his room all day and the day before and the day before that. After a while she went to find her mother.

Mrs. Forbes was in her bindery cooking up a batch of wheat paste. She sat on a stool by the hot plate, stirring. The smell reminded Brooke of kindergarten. She stood just inside the room next to the cartons of law books, remembering what Benji had said about his fainting in school, the way he'd described the looks on the other kids' faces. Mrs. Forbes saw her and smiled. Had he told Mom what he'd told her? She wanted to ask, she wanted to know.

"How's it going, Mom?"

"Fine." Mrs. Forbes wiped the hair away from her face with the back of her hand. "But, oh, how I wish people wouldn't use Scotch tape to repair torn pages. It ruins the paper. I've been doing nothing but corner extensions and invisible mends all day."

"Have you seen Benji?"

"Not since we came back from the library. Why?"

At least he'd been out of his room, thought Brooke. But the library? He had more than enough books already.

"Just wondering. Didn't I go to day camp when I was his age?"

"He doesn't need it. He's perfectly content on his own. In his room. Playing or reading."

"But shouldn't he be outdoors more?"

"If it makes you any happier, I'm planning an all-day picnic at the swimming hole this Saturday. Hmm. Just thinking about it cools me off. Want to invite Izzy?"

Brooke nodded. "But shouldn't he be seeing other kids? He used to all the time."

"He gets enough of them at school. He's happier alone with his books and all his little projects." Mrs. Forbes was stirring faster.

"But, Mom." I should stop, thought Brooke — but she couldn't. "It's like he's hiding up there. And he looks anemic. He looks the way he does in the winter. And it's summer. The middle of summer. And you said he thinks too much."

Mrs. Forbes lifted the pot off the burner and slammed it down on the table.

"You're driving me crazy with these endless third degrees. What's gotten into you? What's brought all this on again? Why can't you leave it be? Let him be happy this summer."

"Okay, Mom, okay. I'm sorry. Don't get so mad. I just wanted to know if he's all right. Really all right."

"He's fine. How many times do I have to tell you? Now, leave me alone, please. I've got to finish up the last of these hymnals."

What is it with her, thought Brooke. Every time I mention Benji she goes into a tailspin and cuts me off. It was so unfair.

Feeling sorry for herself, she went to find some turpentine to clean the dried paint smears off her hands and legs.

The week slipped by. When they finished a storm window, Izzy and Brooke leaned it against the wall of the garage to dry.

"Mom and I figured out how much we've earned. One hundred and seventy-five dollars each, not counting what Dad is going to owe us," Izzy announced. The figure checked with the running total Brooke had been keeping in her head.

"Benji coming to the picnic?" Izzy wanted to know.

"Yeah. Why wouldn't he?"

"No reason. Jason, too, I guess?" said Izzy.

"Uh huh. And Hank and Jud of course. And Ricky."

Izzy made a face. "How'll we all fit in the car? Who's Benji bringing?"

"No one." Brooke hesitated and then dipped her brush into the can of white paint.

"Only four more and we're done," said Izzy after a while. Brooke ran her brush carefully along the edge of the frame. She was trying to remember what Benji had been like during the winter when he'd had friends over, but the past seemed obliterated. There was only the now.

The car bumped and lurched through a tunnel of trees stippled with light that spun and froze and flickered. Brooke could hear the sound of the river off to the left. Then they were in the open.

"Great," said Brooke. "Nobody else is here."

Mr. Forbes parked the car at the far end of the loading area beside the abandoned spool mill. Benji was the first out. The ground was covered with old wood chips. Mr. Forbes lowered the tailgate and freed Jason and his friends and the inflated raft.

"Just dump everything onto the raft, Dad," said Jason. "We'll portage it in."

"Not the food, you won't," said his father.

"And not the thermoses," added his mother. "Take the towels if you want."

"Want to portage me?" asked Izzy.

Ricky groaned. "Hey. Sure," said Jason. "But you gotta lie still."

"Forget it, then," said Izzy. "I'm the bouncy type. I'll walk."

Benji had already climbed the bank ahead of them, following the faint path through the spruce trees. The trail wended its way, skirting rocks and underbrush, along the ridge above the river. Then at the edge of a steep drop, the path stopped as if it had been sheared off, and they slid and scrambled the last few yards.

"Hey, Izz. Get a load of the rafters," said Brooke.

Far behind them they could hear crashing and cursing and branches snapping, and over all the noise, Jason yelling orders.

Ahead of them a pebbly strip of land curved out to a point in the river. Upstream, the water slipped over Bash Bish Falls in thin sheets, not in its usual torrent. There was little foam, and the murmur of the water spilling faded into the background sounds of the day. At the base of the falls the pool spread out with hardly a ripple. Brooke could mark how low the water level was against the stain on the boulders that lined the far bank.

Mr. Forbes set down the picnic baskets. Mrs. Forbes took off her sandals. Brooke and Izzy submerged the watermelon in a hollow of rock carved by the current.

"Watch out below," yelled Jason. The yellow raft came sailing over the edge of the drop-off and blundered down the slope, spraying towels. It caromed to a stop, barely missing Benji, and lay on the pebbles, blubbering.

"Perfect landing, you guys," whooped Jason.

"The towels didn't quite make it," his mother called up to him. "Collect them on the way down. And girls, pile your clothes where they won't get wet."

Brooke and Izzy stripped to their bathing suits and Izzy began to gasp her way into the water, inch by inch. Brooke picked up their cut-offs and tee shirts and carried them to her mother.

"It's freezing! Oh. Oh, jeez, I can't feel my feet," bleated Izzy.

Jason and Hank's clothes were strewn everywhere, all inside out. Rick was working himself out of his pants.

"Oh. I almost forgot. This is for Benji." He pulled a crumpled envelope out of his pocket. It's a birthday invitation, Brooke guessed instantly. A small, square envelope was a dead giveaway. Benji examined it.

"I wonder who's writing me a letter?" he said.

"Open it and see," said Brooke.

Benji turned the envelope over and began to peel the flap off in strips. Watching him made Brooke itchy.

"Here. Let me do it," she offered.

Benji went on shredding until the flap stood up in a tattered fringe. Inside the envelope Brooke could see the top of a shaped card. Benji pulled it out.

"Hey, Brooke, stop stalling!" yelled Izzy. "I'm turning blue!"

"Who's it from?" asked Brooke.

"I don't know yet," Benji said. The card pictured a ballet dancer cut out like a paper doll. On her bright pink tutu in sparkling letters was written "Twirl Away, Whirl Away, Come to My Birthday."

Benji opened the card. At the bottom somebody had outlined in dots the name Rosie Renwick and somebody else had gone over the letters in heavy pencil. The rest of the card was covered with Rs in the same pencil. Some of them were backward.

"It's R-R-R-Rosie," said Benji. "That's the way she always signs her papers at school. Like a running start."

"C'mon, Benji," called Mr. Forbes, "get a move on. Strip down. Into your suit."

"I forgot it," said Benji.

"Forgot? Well, you'll just have to swim in your underpants and wear your shorts home. We've got to practice your dead man's float."

"I don't want to. I don't like swimming."

"Once you learn you'll love it. C'mon, sport." His father flicked a few drops of water in his direction.

Benji backed up. "It's too cold."

"Don't be silly. It's invigorating. Good for you. Gets your circulation moving."

"I always sink," said Benji, "and it's dark down there."

"I'll take him later, Dad," said Brooke.

"Better get it over with now. Stop stalling, Benj."

"No," said Benji. He turned and started up the rocky beach toward the bank.

"Allen." Mrs. Forbes's tone sounded a warning.

"Does he have to swim, Mom?" asked Brooke.

"Not today. Let him go, Allen. He's happier digging in the woods."

Mr. Forbes hesitated, his eyes on Benji. Then he took four running steps and did a flat racer's dive into the water.

"Brooke!" shrieked Izzy. "Are you coming or not? Oh, gross, look at my thighs. I've got goose pimples the size of boils!"

Brooke picked her way over the pebbles and waded out to where Izzy was waiting. The worst part was getting in. Once they were numbed to the cold, they swam to the base of the falls and clung to the rocks, letting their legs lift and swing with the current. Then they swam back and spread their towels and lay in the sun. The boys had lost interest in the raft. Mr. Forbes was doing laps, to the wall of rock on the far shore and back. Benji wandered along the water's edge, picking up stones and carrying them back to a stump on the bank.

Izzy squirmed and sat up. "I'm blotching already," she said. "I can't stand this sunbathing and sweating routine. What's Jason doing with that little plastic football?"

"Playing figgerball, probably," said Brooke without opening her eyes. Then she propped herself up on her elbows and stared past her feet. "Yup. Figgerball. If it isn't soccer, it's figgerball."

"How do you play it?" asked Izzy.

"Depends on where and how many people there are. Jason keeps changing the rules. But there's always a figger — he carries the ball — and if you're not the figger you're a masher. It's utterly point-less."

"Sounds like fun." Izzy stood up, tugging at the bottom of her bathing suit. "Hey, Jason. Can I be on your team?"

Jason dodged out of Hank's grasp and tossed her the ball underhanded. "Run!" he said.

Izzy juggled the ball for a second on her fingertips and then clutched it to her chest. She began to limp and hobble over the pebbles toward the water.

"Not that way!" yelled Jason. "That's the Zone."

"Zone?" Izzy hesitated and then took off for the point, pursued by Jud.

"No, no, you idiot," shouted Ricky. "That's Penalty Point."

Izzy looked wildly about. "Where? Where?" she shouted at Jason.

Hank dashed up behind her. "Flip the ball to me," he said out of the side of his mouth, "and I'll tell you."

"Don't make a deal," bellowed Jason, "or it's a Double Forfeit."

Izzy sprinted toward the bank. "Stop! Stop! Out of bounds!"

There was only one other place to go. Izzy swerved in the direction of Bash Bish Falls. Mrs. Forbes was laying out the pic-nic on an old quilt. "Away from the food," she warned as Izzy galloped near.

Izzy stopped. Suddenly she lofted the ball out toward Mr. Forbes. "A chucker!" she shouted. The football landed with a faint splash and bobbed a few feet from Mr. Forbes's head. "No, it's a rafter. Grab it, Mr. Forbes. That's one hundred and six points for me. I retire." She sank down on the towel next to Brooke. "I see what you mean," she said.

"Told you," said Brooke, rolling over onto her stomach. "You were the best part."

Benji appeared at the edge of the quilt and began to dig about in the picnic basket.

"The food's all out," said his mother. "What are you looking for? If it's Rosie's invitation, I found it. It had slipped under some rocks."

"I'm not going," said Benji. "Did you bring any toothpicks? I want to build a scaling ladder for my gun emplacements."

"What do you mean, you're not going?" asked Brooke.

"He doesn't have to, if he doesn't want to," said her mother, and then to Benji, "I'll call Mrs. Renwick tonight."

Brooke raised herself on her arms and turned to look at him. "But you love birthday parties," she said. "Helium balloons and candles and those games with prizes and everyone wins."

"I don't want to go," said Benji. "Any

toothpicks, Mom?" he repeated.

"When is it?" asked Brooke.

"Lay off, Brooke. He doesn't want to go," said her mother.

"I guess I could use little twigs instead," Benji said to himself after a moment.

Brooke shifted closer to him. Next to her, Izzy's panting had subsided. "But Benji," she whispered, "why don't you want to go? Rosie's okay. Isn't she?"

Benji gave her a straight, blank stare. "They might serve macaroni salad," he said.

" 'Sixty-eight bottles of beer on the wall, sixty-eight bottles of beer. . . .' "

Brooke leaned her head against the back of the seat and closed her eyes. Jason and his cohorts had been singing ever since the car pulled out of the spool mill parking lot, and Izzy was kneeling on the seat, facing backward, singing along with them and snorting like a lunatic.

"Is he asleep?" Brooke heard her father ask.

"Yes."

Brooke opened her eyes a crack. In the front seat Benji was slumped against his mother's arm. Brooke could just see the top of his head.

"About the party," said Mr. Forbes. His voice was low. Brooke strained to hear.

"Maybe we should make him go. People might wonder."

Mrs. Forbes glanced up at the rearview mirror. Brooke lowered her eyelids.

"No. Birthday parties are licensed bedlam, Allen. It might trigger something. Why invite trouble? Everything's going so well. So far, anyway."

"Hadn't thought of that angle."

"Let's just run the summer out. School starts soon enough."

There was a loud burp and a burst of laughter from the back. The singing began again. " 'Sixty-five bottles of beer on the wall. . . .' "

"And then what?" said Mr. Forbes. "And then what?" he repeated. "I swear, if it isn't one thing, it's another."

Brooke felt the car surge forward. She opened her eyes. Her father had veered out to pass the car in front. A truck's coming, thought Brooke. Doesn't he see it? It isn't far enough away. There isn't enough time. But their station wagon hitched into overdrive and then cut back into the right lane. As the truck whipped by them, horn blaring, Brooke found that she was pressing both feet against the floor as hard as she could.

Benji went up to his room as soon as they got home. Mr. Forbes rinsed out the thermoses while Brooke and Izzy helped put away the leftovers and sponged off the plastic lining of the picnic containers. The smell of spilled salad dressing and mayonnaise almost made Brooke gag. There was nothing more disgusting than cleaning up after a picnic. Gnawed chicken bones and slimy pieces of watermelon rind.

"Save the watermelon rinds," said Mrs. Forbes. "I'm going to make pickles."

When they were through, Jason stripped off his tee shirt and began to chin himself on the door frame. Jason never did anything in private, thought Brooke.

"Can I use your hairbrush?" asked Izzy. She tagged after Brooke upstairs.

"I don't know where it is," Brooke said. The day was over. She felt too tired to be polite. She wished Izzy would leave. Water ran in the sink and then Izzy reappeared.

"Got any bobby pins or barrettes or even a headband? I look like a freak," Izzy said.

"Top bureau drawer." Brooke sprawled in the rocking chair.

"What's this?" Izzy held up a piece of white paper. "Is it yours? I didn't know you could type."

"I can't," said Brooke.

"Well, someone typed this. I think it's a poem. Listen. It's titled 'Terrible Things That Happen in War.'"

"Give it to me," said Brooke, coming over to her. "It must be Benji."

"Can I see it, too?"

A few of the words had been canceled with Xs and the type faded in and out. It was Benji's all right. The ribbon on his typewriter was worn. Brooke shared the paper between them and Izzy mouthed the words under her breath.

Wire with posts, here come the tanks and
    here come the hosts.
And when they charge they say a call and
    in wars lots of them fall. And also in
    wars you need lots of things and you
    need more than lots.
You needs tons.
You need tons of guns. There are pigeons
    flying all around.
There are soldiers hiding on the ground.
And this is the time of World War Two. I
    was in that war and so were you.
And that is the skull of me.
I was killed by a box of TNT.

Izzy's voice rose and she turned to look at Brooke with her mouth open. "My gosh, how does he think this stuff up?" she said. "And it's so long."

"There's more," said Brooke. Izzy went back to reading.

But there is no war anymore. There are
   only dead horses and broken-down air
   forces.
And there is one dog, no, there are ten.

"Benji wrote this? Are you sure?" said
Izzy slowly.

"Yes. Usually he leaves them on my pillow." Brooke took the paper back and
folded it in half.

"No wonder he flipped out at school. His
brain must be working overtime," said
Izzy.

She's talking about his fainting again,
thought Brooke. That's twice now. She
wondered if Izzy knew something she
didn't know, and wished that there was a
way she could find out. Without asking.
Absolutely no talking about it, Mom and
Dad had said. To anybody. But they talked
about it, she thought suddenly, with each
other. Trouble, her mother had said, why
ask for trouble. What kind of trouble?

"Let's see if there is any iced tea left,"
she said abruptly. "Then I'll walk you to
the corner."

Later, back in her room, she picked
Benji's typed poem off her bed and read it
again. She didn't like it. That business
about a skull. It was morbid. It didn't make
any sense. She puzzled over the last lines
and then she opened the middle drawer of

her desk and took out an old stationery box. It was filled with scraps of paper. Brooke rifled through them until she found the one she was looking for. It was almost the first poem Benji had ever given her. It was still her favorite. Most of the words were spelled phonetically, and it had taken her a long time to figure it out the first time she had read it. Now she knew it by heart, but she still liked to pretend that she had never seen it before.

"One time," Brooke corrected the spelling and separated the words in her mind as she read, "I was walking down the street. I met a girl. She was, she was beautiful. I kissed her. We fall in love. We lived together."

Benji had told her that the "She was, she was" repeat was a mistake, but Brooke hadn't let him change it.

Chapter 8

Brooke wandered out of the kitchen, eating a second piece of zucchini bread. She felt strangely restless and tired. Usually summer Sundays blended in with the other days of the week, but this one seemed different. It had a tag-end nagging feeling like a winter Sunday that pretended to be peaceful and lazy but underneath was taut with hangings-on and things left undone and things expected of her.

The telephone sat on the hall table, its cord twisted and dangling over the edge. I really ought to call Izzy, thought Brooke, but the storm windows are finished and we don't have anything lined up for next week. I'll wait until later. Tomorrow.

The living room was still cool and shaded, but outside the window, beyond the porch railing and the lawn, the air above Ashpotag Road shimmered and danced in the heat like a swarm of no-see-ums. The pick-up truck was gone. Dad was probably on one of his building-site tours with Jason. Parts of the Sunday newspaper covered the sofa and the coffee table and the floor. Brooke picked up the magazine section and carried it out to the porch. The sun hadn't reached the hammock yet. She settled into it and opened the magazine at random. The cover had looked colorful and interesting, but the inside was all black and white and there was a two-page ad for back-to-school clothes in the middle. Brooke let the magazine drop unread onto her stomach. The leaves on the lowest branch of one of the maples were turning red. Brooke knew that early turning was a sign the tree was dying, but all the other leaves were still green. Even so, the summer was slipping away. It was the second week of August already and she hadn't climbed Stark Mountain or the water tower. She hadn't even hiked on the Long Trail with Benji. I ought to look for my canteen, or find Benji and thank him for his poem. Move, legs, she commanded, but they just lay there. Brooke wiggled a toe to make sure she could still tell her feet what to do.

"Is this one done enough?" said Benji from somewhere behind the house. Brooke couldn't hear anyone answer. Who is he talking to, she wondered.

Blazer! In his barn again, I'll bet. That

experiment. Whatever it is. Brooke pushed the magazine off her lap and climbed out of the hammock and over the porch railing.

"That looks terrific. How about doing the beets next?" Her mother's voice. Brooke slowed and changed direction. She headed toward the garden.

"Have I earned a dollar yet?" asked Benji.

"More like sixty cents."

"I could replant the yellow squash, maybe. The ones Delilah dug up."

"Don't bother. I don't know why I planted them in the first place. Nobody ever eats them. I'll throw them on the compost heap. But you could help me restake the tomato plants. That blasted dog!"

Brooke stopped just short of the corner, in the shade of the house. If Mom sees me she'll make me weed, she thought.

"Does the gas station store sell mousetraps?" asked Benji. "You could get some when you go downtown later. About twelve, or twenty-five." Brooke heard him clear his throat. "You put them all ready to go between the rows and cover them with newspaper. Then when Delilah steps on the paper they go off with a big bang. Louder than party snappers. They're supposed to scare her away. For good. At least it works when you're trying to train dogs to stay off furniture."

"It does? Where did you read that?"

There was a silence. "I heard it somewhere," said Benji finally.

A faint repeated ringing began inside the house. Probably Izzy, thought Brooke. The ringing went on and on.

"Brooke! Can you get that!" yelled Mrs. Forbes.

Brooke was sure Izzy would give up before she got there, but the phone was still ringing when she reached the hall.

"Hello," she said crossly.

"Brooke, dear, is that you?"

"Oh. Hello, Mrs. Gibson. I'll get Mom."

"Don't bother, dear. It's you I want to talk to — and Isabelle." Mrs. Gibson's voice dropped. "About business. This afternoon if possible. It's my only free day."

* * *

Mrs. Gibson was in the middle of her front lawn with Delilah. They were both digging a hole. Mrs. Gibson was turning up clumps of sod with a spade, and dirt flew out between Delilah's hind legs. Nearby were three other finished holes surrounded by pyramids of earth. The lawn looked as if it had been bombed.

"What are you looking for, Mrs. Gibson?" asked Izzy. "Buried treasure?"

"I'm not looking. I'm planting. It's the only way to keep Delilah from tearing up the grass here." Mrs. Gibson rested on the handle of her shovel. "We're going to re-landscape the spot with some bushes. She's helping me plant her out, aren't you, you good, good girl?"

I hope she didn't get us over here to plant, thought Brooke. Planting is as bad as weeding. "What did you want to see us about, Mrs. Gibson?" she asked.

"Oh, yes. The garage."

"Take five, Delilah," said Izzy. Delilah went into another frenzy of digging. Brooke and Izzy followed Mrs. Gibson.

"As you can see, I'm peeling," announced Mrs. Gibson, pointing at the wall of her garage. "All over. And I've got leaks. Around my windows."

Fantastic! thought Brooke. She wants us to paint. The whole thing. It's a huge job. It'll take the rest of the summer. Mrs. Gibson was saying something about scraping off the old paint first and personal liability.

"I don't want either of you working here in bare feet. Bare feet are not safe," she said, "and I presume you have your own ladders and equipment."

"Yes. Except for the paint. We don't supply that," Brooke told her.

"Not white." Mrs. Gibson frowned at the garage wall. "I'm tired of white. Something new and zippy. Red. I'll buy it through your father." Mrs. Gibson addressed the last to Izzy.

I'll earn a mint, thought Brooke. Much too much to keep in my bureau drawer under my underpants. I'll have to open an account at the bank. "There's one other thing, Mrs. Gibson," she said. "We've raised our rates. Remember? It was on our ad. It's two fifty an hour this summer."

"Each?"

"We're older and more experienced."

Mrs. Gibson considered for a moment and then nodded. "Fair enough. I heard from the Pritchards that you were thorough and tidy. I like tidy painters. When can you start?"

"Tomorrow?" said Brooke. "On the scraping."

"Good," said Mrs. Gibson, "and by the by, since you happen to be here, would the two of you mind carrying these azaleas out to the front for me and setting them in the holes?"

There were four bushes lined up like bowling pins outside the garage door, their roots balled and bound in burlap. Delilah was sniffing at them.

"Mrs. Gibson always manages a freebie," Brooke whispered to Izzy.

On her way home, Brooke's mind was

on money. She walked slowly, figuring in her head. It would take until Labor Day to finish the garage, so six hours a day times two fifty an hour, times five days a week times four weeks . . . Brooke stopped with one hand raised and looked up to find a clear place to visualize the problem against, but her eyes never reached the sky.

Benji was on the roof outside his room. His back was toward her and he was struggling to unhook the screen from one of his windows. It was half off already and hanging askew. As she watched, he bent his knees to get a better grip on the frame and braced his black sneakers against the shingles. The screen was almost as big as he was. Oh, no! thought Brooke. He might slip, or fall if the thing comes off with a jerk. Where was Mom? But it was too late to yell. She saw the screen come loose and sway out over Benji's head. He staggered for a moment and then managed to lean it back against the wall of the house. Through his tee shirt Brooke could see the sharp points of his shoulder blades. He stood looking at the screen for a moment and then he picked it up, tilted it, and pushed it through the open window.

"What are you doing?" Brooke called to him.

Astride the sill, Benji turned and

scanned the lawn until he spotted her. Then he raised a finger to his lips and slid out of sight. The window shut with a bang.

The *Do Not Disturb* sign was still hanging on his doorknob. Oh no, thought Brooke, it's not stopping me this time. She knocked once to warn him and barged into the room. Benji was dragging the screen across the rug.

"What are you doing?" she repeated.

Benji hesitated. "Isn't my sign up out there?"

"Why'd you take that screen off? Will you tell me that? You want to inundate the place with bugs?" Benji rested the screen against the bedpost. "The fireflies weren't so bad, but mosquitoes . . . And moths. Bleeech!" Brooke shuddered. "I can't stand soft moths."

"Lift up the mattress, will you, Brooke," said Benji. "I want to get rid of this thing. Mom would find it if I just put it under the bed."

"You could always put it back on the window," said Brooke, but she heaved up the bottom half of the mattress for him. "C'mon, Benji. Give. What are we doing this for?"

"A little higher," said Benji. "There."

Brooke let the mattress flop back. Benji retucked the blankets and straightened out the bedspread until it hung evenly. "You can't tell a thing," he said. Then he crossed the room and closed the door. "Where's Mom?"

"Haven't a clue. What's Mom got to do with it?"

"Nothing, I hope," said Benji, "but I've got to think up a way to keep her out of here."

"Why?" asked Brooke. "What's there to see?"

Benji stared at her intently, as if he were trying to hold her gaze. Brooke looked away and let her eyes wander across his office, his bureau, toward the window. She stopped. Her head snapped back. There were holes in the side of the door of his office. Freshly drilled holes. A dozen of them, or more. And on the floor next to a stack of library books were a brace and bit. Air holes, thought Brooke, like the ones you punch in the lids of jars.

"Okay, Benji. What's in the office?"

Benji cleared his throat. "First you've got to promise not to tell, anyone, even Izzy."

"Okay," said Brooke. "I promise. But what is it?"

"Wait! And promise to help me keep it a secret from Mom and Dad?"

"I'll try," said Brooke. "But you'd better

put that drill back in the shop or Dad will hit the ceiling. And vacuum up that sawdust, too."

Benji moved toward the door of his box. He rubbed the toe of his sneaker through the trickle of sawdust that trailed around the base, trying to make it vanish into the rug. The loop on the combination lock hung open. Benji unhooked it.

"Stay still," he whispered, flipping back the latch. "And whatever you do, don't scream."

Chapter 9

With a last warning look, Benji opened the
door, a bit at a time, trying not to make
any noise. Brooke moved in beside him. She
was close enough to see, but far enough
back to be out of the way in case whatever
it was came out leaping or snarling or,
worse, slithering. Like one of those huge
garden snakes slashed with yellow rings
that were supposed to be harmless. But
there was nothing on the floor of the box
except a worn piece of blue rug she'd never
seen before. The rug lapped up an inch or
so at the side.

What else had he added, she wondered.
Benji leaned in. He seemed to be searching.
Brooke peered over his head. Not much.
There wasn't room. She could see the en-
tire interior at a glance.

The toy chest took up the whole of one
wall. On it was the typewriter, flagged with
a fresh sheet of paper, and next to that a
Snoopy mug with pencils and Magic Mark-
ers and a ruler sticking out of it. An old

goose-necked lamp arched over a pile of pads and loose papers. Brooke remembered the lamp. It used to be in her mother's bindery.

The red wastepaper basket, bottom end up, had been drawn as close to the desk as it would go. On top of it for a cushion was the tooth-fairy pillow she'd made him last Christmas. What did he do with his knees when he typed, Brooke wondered. They must stick out like elbows. The office was so small. But so cozy, so perfect. Brooke wanted to get in it. She figured she could fit if she scrunched.

"I can't find him," whispered Benji.

"Find what?"

"Lucifur." He craned his neck and his head swiveled.

"Lucifur who?" Brooke bent forward without moving her feet.

The sides of the box were rough and unfinished and had been reinforced all the way around with strips of wood. They formed a narrow shelf. On it was a row of plastic soldiers, a pencil sharpener, a mashed and twisted tube of modeling glue, some scaly dinosaurs, a stapler, a shriveled apple core.

"There," Benji breathed. "There he is."

"Where?"

Benji pointed to a knothole on the back wall, high and to the left, near the corner.

No, not a knothole, Brooke realized. A mitten. A tiny dark-brown woolen mitten, newborn-baby size, hanging on the wall.

"What is it?" Brooke whispered.

"It's my bat," said Benji. "My little brown bat."

"Oh!" said Brooke. She put a hand over her mouth, but a stifled sound escaped. The brown mitten gave a twitch.

"Don't scream. He won't hurt you," said Benji. "He's asleep."

The bat twitched again.

"No, he isn't." Brooke stepped back. "He's moving."

Two pale brown-gray ovals materialized at the bottom of the fur puffball and fanned forward. The movement was as slight as a shiver.

"Sssh," said Benji. "He hears us."

They're ears, thought Brooke. Of course. Bats hang upside down.

The ears flickered and the bit of fur between them lifted out and up. Brooke found herself looking into a miniature mouse face and two bright eyes, pinpoints of glistening black.

"Go back to sleep, Lucifur," Benji crooned. "It isn't time yet."

The ears wavered. They're like tiny petals, thought Brooke. Lucifur was staring right at her. He gave a little squeak. It sounded cheerful and questioning.

"Not yet," Benji repeated firmly. He shut the door. "I don't want him to wake up now," he said to Brooke.

Brooke was still looking at the blank wall of the closed door. A bat. She couldn't believe how small it was.

"Where did you get him? When did you get him?" she asked finally.

"From Noah's barn. This morning."

"You mean that man gave it to you?"

Benji cleared his throat. "No. I found him myself. Hanging all alone. I guess his mother had left him because he's not a baby anymore. But I wanted him. And when I touched him he didn't mind. He liked me." Benji drew a breath. "So I took him."

He sounded so solemn that she wanted to reach out and touch his hair, but he moved away from her to latch and lock his box.

"You won't tell, will you?" There was a new tone in his voice, a tone that Brooke had never heard before. Fierce. "You promised!"

Brooke didn't know what to answer. A bat. Why would anyone want one? They were scary. People were petrified of them. What had Sam Renwick said in the kitchen? "Kill 'em first, ask questions later."

But it was obvious that Benji loved that bat already, she thought. It's almost as if he has to have him. And Lucifur looked so little and harmless — just a bit of brown fluff, small enough to live in a dollhouse.

"No," she said at last. "I won't tell. But what are you going to do with him? How are you going to feed him? Won't he die in there?"

"Don't worry. I've got it all figured out."

"Supper!" Their mother's voice echoing up the stairs startled them both.

"Will he be all right? Can we leave him?" asked Brooke.

"As long as we're back by dark," answered Benji. "That's when he eats."

"Did anyone hear me?" Mrs. Forbes called again. "I said supper."

"Coming," Brooke called back. "What does he eat?"

"Bugs." Benji picked up the drill. "I'll return this to Dad's toolbox."

Usually Benji picked and played with his food. He would cut his meat into squares and triangles and decorate each piece with bits of vegetable or potato or radish from his salad. But tonight he ate like one of those speeded-up people in a silent movie. Brooke couldn't keep up with him.

"I'm through," he announced. He'd beaten her by half a slice of ham.

"You can't be!" His mother sounded shocked. "I've barely begun." She checked his plate.

"I was hungry," said Benji. "But now I'm stuffed. I'll clear."

Brooke hid the rest of her ham under her knife. "I'll help," she said.

"Are there seconds, Mom?" asked Jason. "Hey! What happened to my plate?"

"You're getting fat," Brooke told him.

"No, I'm not," protested Jason. He sucked in his breath and looked down at his stomach. "That's all muscle."

Benji's head bobbed up next to the arm of his father's chair. "Hold it. What's going on here? Leave me my salad," said Mr. Forbes, elbowing him off.

"At least it's a pleasant change to see them pitch in without being asked." Mrs. Forbes snagged a last forkful before Benji whipped her plate away. The jar of mustard relish was under his arm.

In the kitchen Brooke cautioned him. "Slow down. They'll get suspicious."

"Can't." Benji dumped the dishes in the sink. He opened the freezer. "Look outside."

The light was fading.

Benji stabbed at the ice cream with a spoon. "This stuff is hard as rock. I can't make a dent in it."

"Take it to Dad," said Brooke. "He can serve."

"I'm not having any," said Benji.

"I won't either, then."

"Well, this is original," said Mr. Forbes. "Ice cream with salad." He looked at the carton. "Real peach. No additives. What's coming next?"

"There are only three bowls," said Jason. "Where's mine?"

"We're not having any," said Brooke. "I'll take that salad plate for you, Dad. Come on, Benji."

The sawdust, Brooke remembered. "I'll get the vacuum," she told Benji when they were back in the kitchen. She rummaged in the broom closet by the icebox. "You take this. I'll handle the rest."

Benji wrestled the hose attachment up the stairs. The metal nozzle bumped on each step. "What's going on out there?" called Mrs. Forbes.

"Its okay, Mom," answered Brooke.

"Plug it in," Benji said as soon as the door to his room was shut. "You start cleaning. I'll get things ready."

He went into the bathroom and came back with a glass of water. Brooke had turned on the vacuum and was sucking up the sawdust. Benji put the glass on his worktable and opened one of the drawers. He took out an eyedropper. Brooke wandered across the room pointing the nozzle at a few dead flies and a paper clip. The clip rattled up the hose.

"I've done the whole room," she said, turning the machine off.

Benji had raised the screenless window as high as it would go and removed the shade from the lamp. He switched it on.

"Don't do that," said Brooke. "You'll let in all the bugs."

"I know," said Benji. "That's the point." The bulb glared, but the light didn't go very far. Benji switched it off. "Darn," he said. "It still isn't dark enough. We'll have to wait."

They sat cross-legged on the floor watching the clock. The twilight moved into the room.

"Now," said Benji at last. "Get the light and the one by my bed, too." He turned the switch on the worktable lamp.

It was as if bugs of every kind had been lined up outside waiting. In a minute, moths fluttered around the lights, bumping and ricocheting off the bulbs. The air whined with mosquitoes.

"I'm being eaten alive," said Brooke.

"Okay. That's enough." Benji closed the window. "Turn off the lights." There were squeaks from inside the office. "Good," Benji said. "He's ready. Now I'll see if he'll catch indoors. Sometimes they won't."

"What if he doesn't?" whispered Brooke.

"I bought cream cheese and baby food this afternoon with my weeding money.

Just in case. It's downstairs. In the icebox. Way in back. Meal-worm larvae would be better. I asked, but the dumb gas station store didn't know what I was talking about." Benji fumbled with the lock in the dusk and opened the door.

Lucifur came out like an arrow, his wings stretched and thrumming. Flying, he looked gigantic. Not the same little bat. Benji ducked to the side. Brooke was terrified. She dropped to the floor with her arms over her head.

"He's doing it, I think," said Benji. "Oh, boy! Oh, boy! Look at him go!"

Brooke raised her head cautiously, both hands still covering her hair. A streak, a boomerang, a black *W* darted here and there, turning and twisting, diving and climbing, spiraling and zigzagging. Benji's fists were clenched. He was rigid with excitement.

"He must be doing it! There! I'm sure he got one!"

Brooke gaped upward. Lucifur jetted toward the wall, but at the last moment peeled off and away.

"I think he got another," said Benji proudly.

"How do you know?" Except for the moths, the insects were too small to see.

"Because of the way he's flying," said Benji. "But I wish he'd chase a moth. Then

I could be sure. There. There's one, Lucifur. He hears it. Oh, shoot, he missed."

"He's so fast, Benji. I can barely follow him."

"He'll get a lot faster. When he's had more chance to practice. He's only about two months old, you know."

They watched in silence for a while. Brooke's heart had calmed down. She was getting used to his flying.

"How long has he been out?" Benji asked once.

"Ten minutes. Maybe more," Brooke guessed. She felt as if she were watching a crazy tennis match. Her head was going every which way, trying to keep track of Lucifur. The deepening darkness made it harder. He was a shade among shadows. Then suddenly she couldn't find him anymore.

"Where is he?" she asked. "What happened to him?"

"It's okay, I think. Turn on the lights."

"You turn them on."

"Now," said Benji. "Help find him. No, not under the bed. Higher up. But not hanging free. He likes his tummy to the wall or something solid."

They both searched, but it was Benji who found him. He was hanging from the head cap of a book on the top shelf of Benji's bookcase.

"Smart bat," said Benji. "That's one of my best books. It's his night roost," he explained to Brooke.

Brooke could see Lucifur's feet, all toes, tiny and as fine as pine needles, hooked over the curved edge of the book's spine. His wings had disappeared completely. He was a minuscule fur ball again.

"What's a night roost?"

Lucifur was swinging, first from one foot and then from the other.

"Where he rests between feedings. But he should have water." Benji knelt by the open door of his office and reached under the blue carpet. When he turned around, his hands shone silvery. He was wearing the thermal liners to his ski gloves.

"Why are you wearing those?" asked Brooke.

"All scientists do," said Benji. "He's wild."

"Does he bite?"

"No. Not unless he has to. Sometimes he nibbles, but you can barely feel it. Now, lift me up. I can't reach him."

When Brooke set Benji down again, Lucifur was cowering in the cupped palm of Benji's left hand. Benji's silvered fingers curled over the bat's back. He carried him to the worktable and picked up the eyedropper. It clinked against the rim of the glass.

"He could drink from a saucer, but I'm training him to come when I call," said Benji, clinking again.

There were bugs everywhere. Brooke slapped at her arm. Lucifur's ears seemed to expand and he trembled in Benji's gloved hand.

"You scared him," said Benji. Lucifur's mouth was wide open and he was chittering frantically. Brooke saw a set of teeth, very white, very sharp — shark teeth, but as small as grains of sand. Benji clinked the eyedropper one last time, filled it, and aimed for Lucifur's mouth. A drop of water landed on Lucifur's nose. He stuck out a tiny red tongue and licked it off. Then he sneezed. It was the smallest sneeze Brooke had ever heard. Another drop formed at the end of the eyedropper. Lucifur raised his head. Now he resembled a toy dog and his wings had turned into arms. At least that's what they looked like to Brooke. Exactly like arms. He was bracing himself on them.

Benji squeezed out another drop of water. Lucifur slurped it up and licked his lips. He had stopped trembling. Instead he began to murmur contentedly. Then he yawned.

"I guess he's had enough," said Benji, stashing the eyedropper back in the drawer.

"Are you going to put him back on the book?"

"No. He'll have to night-roost in my office. It's too risky out here. Mom comes to say good night."

Brooke watched him open the door of the box a crack and stick his arm in for an instant.

"He took off," Benji reported. "The moment I let go. I hope he'll sleep."

"Benji, the bugs. We've got to get rid of them," said Brooke. "Bet the vacuum cleaner would work." Zapping the bugs, she decided after a while, was almost the best part. She looped the flexible hose over her shoulder and aimed the nozzle like a gun. The moths were duck soup. She picked them off one by one. But the mosquitoes were fast and tricky and hard to spot. Brooke dragged the vacuum around the room waving the nozzle wildly until Benji told her to stop.

"You're keeping Lucifur up," he said, "and he feeds again later. After he's digested. I'm going to get into my pajamas." He handed her the glass of water. "Can you put this away? I don't want Mom to see it."

Moths fluttered against the mirror over the sink. I forgot to do the bathroom, thought Brooke. Thank goodness my door was closed.

Chapter 10

"Why did you name him Lucifur?" Brooke asked the next night. "Oh, I know. Because of that firefly stuff." They were sitting on the floor of Benji's room, watching Lucifur bug-hunting above their heads. He had discovered the bathroom on a reconnaissance flight. The door on Brooke's side remained closed, but Benji's was open and Lucifur banked in and out.

"Luciferin? No. I never thought of that. It's because his real name, his Latin name, is *Myotis lucifugus.*" Benji spelled it slowly. "I dropped the end part and added an R. I could have called him Gus, I guess. Or Fu. I almost called him that."

"Phoo? I don't like it," said Brooke.

"I know. But it would have fit."

"Why?" asked Brooke.

"*Fu* is the Chinese word for bat. It also means happiness and good luck and something else good, but I've forgotten." Lucifur had taken a break. Benji got up and turned on the lights. This time they found him night-roosting from the ceiling molding above Benji's bed.

"How are we going to get him down from there?" asked Brooke.

"I could climb on your shoulders," Benji said doubtfully.

Lucifur wasn't paying any attention to them. He was busy grooming himself. Twisting his head and contorting his body, he licked the fur on his stomach and back and under his chin. After he'd finished one side he paused and then started on the other, unhurried and fastidious. When he'd done both sides of himself from top to bottom he started all over again.

Then he began on his wings, lapping and kneading every joint; tugging and stretching the rubbery membrane like Jason playing with his sling shot. When both wings were done, he tucked himself up and began on his left foot. It is going to go on forever, thought Brooke.

"I know how to get him down," said Benji. He picked up the eyedropper and tinked on the water glass. Lucifur stopped in mid-lick to listen. Benji clinked again. His hands, in the silvery gloves, sparkled.

"It'll never work," said Brooke. Benji tinked again. Lucifur let go and dropped, spreading his wings at the same moment, and flew straight at Benji's face. It was all over in a flash, like a magic trick. Benji barely had time to jerk his head away before Lucifur was hanging from the collar of his shirt. He'd landed by twist-flipping or somersaulting sideways. Brooke wasn't sure which. It had been so fast.

"He came!" said Benji triumphantly. "Did you see that!" Lucifur hitched down the front of Benji's shirt as fast as he could go and scrambled out onto the worktable. There he crouched, his head up and his mouth open, like a baby bird waiting to be fed. There was no doubt about it. He knew what was coming.

"I've trained him," said Benji, squeezing the eyedropper. "I've trained him." A trained bat. Probably the first ever, thought Brooke. People would pay to see him. We could charge admission. But Benji wouldn't admit anyone. Not even Izzy.

"Benji, about Izzy," said Brooke when Lucifur was back in the box. "I couldn't let her come home after work today because I had to see what Lucifur was doing. I think that hurt her feelings. So, I'm going to tell her. Okay? She won't blab. Honest. I'll make her swear."

"No!" Benji spun around, his voice hard. "Not Izzy. Not anyone. You promised." His back was against the door of the office as if to protect it. He looks cornered, thought

Brooke, like an animal at bay, and for a fleeting moment she was almost afraid of him. Then his shoulders drooped and he seemed to shrink.

"Please," he begged. "If they find out, they'll take him away."

"All right. All right," Brooke said. "If it means that much to you, I'll ditch her somehow."

But as the week wore on, ditching Izzy made Brooke more and more uncomfortable. She knew Izzy didn't buy her excuses and Brooke didn't blame her. She wouldn't have bought them either and she didn't like selling them. Lies piled on top of the secret until she had to be careful about everything she said.

By Thursday afternoon they were two-thirds through with the scraping, but they were scraping in silence. Izzy hadn't been waiting on the corner that morning. She had already signed in on Mrs. Gibson's time sheet and was hard at work when Brooke got there. Delilah bounded about as usual, delirious with joy at having company, but Izzy only nodded at Brooke and didn't offer to help move the extension ladder into position. Feeling strained and embarrassed, Brooke batted Delilah away and climbed up under the eaves. She liked being up high, higher than everybody and everything, on a level with the trees and with only an occasional cloud coasting by above her. It made her feel better. It was peaceful and removed. When Mrs. Gibson pulled into the driveway on one of her periodic inspection trips "between clients," it was Izzy who had to deal with her suggestions.

Poor Izzy. She had to deal with Delilah, too. Except for brief forays to check out the new azalea bushes on the front lawn, Delilah spent all her time sniffing at Izzy's crotch or cavorting around her legs trying to persuade her to play.

"You're getting paint chips in my hair."

Brooke stopped scraping. "Sorry," she said. "Want me to move my ladder?"

"Don't bother," said Izzy. "I'll start on the other side. Drop dead, Delilah!" Brooke watched Izzy stalk off.

There were several swallows' nests tucked under the overhang of the room. The eggs were long since hatched and the baby birds gone, but swallows still wheeled and called in the air around the garage. They reminded Brooke of Lucifur. And Lucifur was the whole trouble. It wasn't that she thought about him all the time, but at four o'clock she wanted to get home to see what he was up to. If only she could have taken Izzy, or explained to her, or gone for a bike ride with her, or a movie, or to her house for supper. But she couldn't. She couldn't stand missing out on anything. What if she hadn't seen the way he landed? It wouldn't have been the same hearing it secondhand, even from Benji. And Lucifur was waking up earlier and earlier. The one time she'd gone with Izzy for a creamy, she'd missed half his feeding. Brooke went back over the week in her mind. That was Tuesday, the day Lucifur went off bugs.

She'd left Izzy at the creamy stand and was home by five. But the door of the box was already open, and inside, Lucifur was eating. Like a dog. Out of a dish. The pink soap dish from the bathroom.

"I got too bitten by mosquitoes. So I decided to try him on the food I bought," Benji explained.

"Couldn't you have at least waited for me?" asked Brooke.

Benji cleared his throat. "You forgot to close my door," he said.

"No, I didn't."

"I didn't hear it click. And he can squeeze through cracks that aren't even there."

Lucifur was crouched on the blue carpet next to the wastebasket. He tipped to look at her and murmured deep in his throat. Then he attacked his dinner again, chittering between bites.

"I couldn't find mealworms, so that's baby tapioca he's eating now. He's already guzzled the cream cheese," said Benji.

"What's that other goop?" asked Brooke.

"Junior Turkey Noodle Dinner. That's all they had. I didn't think he'd like egg yolks or prunes."

Lucifur was trying to lick the far side of the dish but the dish was too wide for him. With his wings folded he was the size of a little bar of guest soap.

"I think he's growing. I'd really like to weigh him. I wish there was such a thing as a teeny-weeny scale," said Benji. "But," his face brightened, "I've got a ruler."

Benji held Lucifur in his gloved hands while Brooke measured him.

"About two-and-a-half inches long," she said, "without his tail."

"Write it down. On the pad by my type-writer. How long *with* his tail?"

"Four inches on the dot. More or less," said Brooke.

"Write it down. Now. We have to measure his wings. I don't think he'll mind," said Benji.

Lucifur minded like crazy. He struggled and shrieked at them. He was livid with rage. Brooke was so terrified she kept dropping the ruler.

"Hurry up," Benji panted.

"Nine and a half. Maybe ten. Somewhere around there."

Benji let go. Lucifur flew into the office and flip-turned onto his perch high in the left-hand corner. There he hung, complaining bitterly. After a while he began to clean himself with a slow, reproachful tongue.

"It was worth it," said Benji. "Write down wingspread, ten. Then write full grown."

"You mean that's as big as he's going to get?"

"Yup."

Lucifur extended his wings and flapped violently, as if reminding them how badly he'd been treated. Then, with a last aggrieved screech, he settled down to nap. "Well, at least we won't have to measure him again," said Brooke, relieved. "He acted as if we were killing him."

"I don't blame him," said Benji. "How would you like it if some giant person held you up by your fingers?"

It sounded like a medieval torture. "I'd hate it," said Brooke, "but we're not talking about fingers. We're talking about wings."

"Wings? Those aren't wings. Everyone just calls them that. Those are his hands!"

"Hands? That's insane. You can't fly with hands!"

"You have to, if you're a mammal," said Benji, "or with your paws." Then he grinned at her. His loose tooth dangled. "Unless you're a whale, of course. Then you'd use your flippers. A whale blimp. You probably wouldn't even be able to get off the water." He cleared his throat. "Nope. Bats are the only flying mammals in the whole history of the world and they fly with their hands. They've been doing it for at least sixty million years. With plain, ordinary hands. Just like ours. Look. I'll show you." He pulled off his gloves, took a pencil out of the Snoopy mug, and picked up the pad of paper. Closing the door on Lucifur, he went over to his worktable. "I'm not such a good drawer," he said after a while, "so I labeled everything."

Benji's diagram was so clear that Brooke couldn't understand why she hadn't figured it out for herself. There was a definite forearm and a wrist and then a tiny, hooked thumb and four long fingers radiating out. She'd noticed those black etched lines when he groomed himself. It was the thin skin connecting them that had fooled her. No wonder when Lucifur first crouched in Benji's hand she'd thought he was resting on arms. He was.

Suddenly she remembered the picture of Icarus in her fourth-grade book of myths, the feathers of his fake wings coming unglued in the heat of the sun. Icarus intoxicated by the feeling of flying, soaring up and up. Down was easy. The secret, she realized, was to be able to go up. Icarus had done it, but Icarus didn't count. He was imaginary and even in a fantasy he had died trying. People can only really do it in airplanes or rockets, she thought, and that's not flying. That's riding.

"Who would believe it," she said to Benji. "Maybe people hate bats so much because they don't know about them."

"They don't want to know about them," said Benji. "They're scared of them and nobody wants to know about things that they're scared of. But you're not scared of me, Lucifur, are you? And I'm not scared of you." Benji turned in his chair. "I hope he won't stay mad," he said.

But Lucifur seemed to have forgotten the whole incident. Later that night he chattered cheerfully over a second helping of cream cheese and then he swung lazily from his perch in the corner of Benji's office, amusing himself. He stretched first one wing and then the other over his head and peeped out at them from underneath like a baby playing peek-a-boo with a blanket.

"Silly bat," said Benji fondly. "Silly old bat."

Brooke reached up a tentative finger and touched Lucifur's fur. It was as light and soft as a whisper of warm wind against her skin. She stroked him again and again.

The next afternoon she had dug out her ski glove liners and dared to hold him for the first time. He stayed quite still in her hand. He was so weightless. Only a fraction of an ounce. An airmail letter that could fly by itself. She looked at her thighs and knees. A few ounces of me wouldn't be worth anything, she thought. That was the most amazing part about him: not that he'd turned out to be cute instead of revolting, but that he could be so little and yet so clever. More than clever. So advanced. She could feel his bones, as fragile as splinters. A minuscule nothing, staring up at her warily, that she could crush by closing her hand. A little nothing that could crawl down walls and catch bugs in the dark and fly like a whiz. She had regarded him with respect.

Delilah's barking interrupted her remembering. For a moment Brooke didn't know where she was. She looked at the scraper in her hand with surprise and then went back to work. On the garage wall beside her, a distorted shadow ladder stretched next to the one she was on. The sun had shifted. She wondered what time it was.

"Izzy?" No answer. Brooke climbed down and went around the corner of the garage. "Izz, what's the time?"

"How should I know." Izzy's scraper made a harsh sound against the clapboards.

"I'll check the clock inside." It was five of four. No point moving the ladder over. "It's almost four," Brooke reported. "Think I'll sign out. I have to go."

"Cramps again? Or do you have to clean your closet?" Izzy flicked at the sill with a cloth to dislodge the last loose paint chips. "Sign me out, too. I gotta rush home and curl my hair."

"Izzy. Don't say things like that."

"Why not?" Izzy turned on her. "You've been saying things like that all week. To avoid me. It's so obvious. Why don't you give it to me straight? Why all the pussy-footing? Why don't you come right out and tell me that you don't want to be friends anymore?"

"But, I do. We are. It's not that . . . It's just. . . ." Brooke stopped.

"Yeah? Just what?" Izzy ran her hand over her hair, forgetting she was still holding the cloth. It left a dusting of paint chips. "Did I do something? What is it? I've been racking my brains. Is it because of Jason? Because I sort of like him and you think that's stupid? You think I acted like a dip at the picnic? Well, I can't help it. He's cute . . . and, I don't know, funny." Brooke shook her head dumbly. Izzy plunged on. "Or is it you've got another best friend that you're hiding from me? Oh, what does it matter. I don't care anymore."

Izzy had run down. Her arms hung at

her sides as if the scraper and cloth were too heavy to lift. Brooke couldn't stand it.

"It's not that, Izzy," she said. "Not any of that. It's not you at all. I'd tell you, I really would. Right now, if I could, but I made a promise. I promised Benji."

"Benji? What does Benji have to do with this? I've hardly laid eyes on him all summer. I don't know whether he's dead or alive."

"He's fine," said Brooke. "But I have to . . . talk to him. Give me one more day. Please? Maybe only a few hours to fix it. Okay? Please? Then I'll explain everything."

"It's not me, really? Really, Brookie? You mean it?"

"I promise. Here, let me get the paint chips out of your hair. Bend down."

"I was beginning to get used to them," said Izzy. "I thought they made me look better."

"You'd look good no matter what," said Brooke. "There. I've got most of it out."

"Maybe Mike could give us a driving lesson tomorrow when he gets off work," Izzy offered. "Shall I ask him?"

"You can ask," said Brooke, "but when I tell you about the secret, I don't think you're going to want to go anywhere."

Chapter 11

Brooke banged through the screen door. There were voices in the kitchen.

"Brooke? That you?" called her mother. "Want some iced tea?"

Reluctantly Brooke went as far as the doorway. Her mother had a pitcher in her hands and her father was getting glasses down from the cupboard. Sam stood by the kitchen table. "Hi, gorgeous," he greeted her.

Mrs. Forbes beamed at him. "Sam's come to do my bindery shelves," she said. "The answer to my prayers. Better than rain in the middle of this drought." She decorated Sam's glass with a slice of lemon and handed it to him.

"The boss said you were raising Cain," said Sam, "so I thought I'd better get over here."

"It's shelves I need, and cubbies, the kind Benji and Rosie have in their classroom, and a new enlarged work area."

Brooke left them talking and went upstairs. She knocked on Benji's door twice and then twice more, their code knock. After a moment she opened the door just wide enough to slip through, in case Lucifur was out and flying. The room was deserted, but there were sloshing sounds from the bathroom.

Benji was bent double over the bathtub. His bottom stuck up in the air and his arms were buried in mountains of soapsuds. The tub was piled and peaked with white foam, and glaciers slid over the side and down onto the floor.

"Oh, good. Brooke." Benji had suds on his chin and nose and frosting his bangs. "Your arm is longer. Pull the plug for me. I've lost the rug and my boat and all my stuffed animals."

He looked so funny and familiar, thought Brooke. Exactly the way he'd looked the time she made the angel food cake for the eighth-grade dance. She'd let him help and by mistake he lifted the electric beater out of the egg whites without turning the motor off.

She felt for the plug through the suds. There was a muffled gurgling and the suds settled, but they didn't seem to be draining away. "Is this my bubble bath? Did you use it all?"

Benji coughed. "My office rug was really dirty. Bat wee and poop."

"Oh, yuk." Brooke fished something out of the foam.

"I think this must be your bear," she said, "or else it's a yeti."

"I don't have a yeti. Maybe it's Rabbit. I can't tell."

Brooke threw it back. It made a hole down through the suds. "We'll have to turn on the shower and wait." She closed the curtain and reached for the cold water tap. Water drummed in the tub. The empty bottle of bubble bath lay in the sink. Brooke dropped it into the wastebasket. "Hey! You used my shampoo, too?"

"There wasn't much left. I tried it first. It didn't work very well."

"Darn it all, Benji. That stuff is expensive. I ought to make you buy me another bottle."

"I can't. I don't have any money. And besides, I need more food for Lucifur."

Brooke regarded him thoughtfully.

"Tell you what," she said. "I'll make a deal with you. As soon as I've gotten rid of the soapsuds for you and rinsed out all the stuff for you and hung it up to dry and wiped the floor before it leaks through to the bindery on top of Mom and Dad and Sam, I'm going downtown and maybe I'll take you with me. Who knows, I might even lend you some money."

"You mean, go right now? This afternoon?" Benji's eyebrows lifted hopefully.

"Yes. To buy more shampoo and food for Lucifur. But . . . I'll only do it if, and it isn't really an 'if,' Benji" — she paused — "if you'll let me tell Izzy. I've got to."

Benji's eyebrows fell and he frowned. "She'll shriek. I know she will." He looked down at his arms. The soap had dried to a film. "She'll be scared and she'll think I'm weird."

"No! She won't, Benji. She likes you. She thinks you're neat. And she'll love Lucifur. You can teach her."

"Can you go to the supermarket? They have a whole aisle of baby food."

"Yes." At least he hadn't said no yet.

"And could you get a big package of cream cheese?"

"Sure. I'm loaded."

The water was still pelting into the tub.

"Okay," said Benji. "Izzy can come. But not today. Tomorrow. And nobody else. Ever."

Done, thought Brooke. It will be even more fun with three of us.

"Can you go right now?" Benji asked.

"Sure. Turn off the water and get your sneakers."

Benji cleared his throat. "I'm not going."

"What? We had it all planned."

"I can't," said Benji.

"Why can't you?"

"The supermarket smells. It makes me feel sick."

"So breathe through your mouth."

"Then people will look at me. Funny." Benji wrung out Bear's legs and wedged him between the towel rack and the wall. The legs hung down, still twisted.

"You go," he said. "Please."

Chapter 12

Late the next afternoon Brooke swore Izzy to secrecy one more time in front of Benji's *Do Not Disturb* sign. Then, when the door had been opened to Brooke's code knock, Izzy, all on her own, swore again to Benji. Benji listened, silent and wary. He still doesn't trust her, Brooke thought, afraid that he might be having second thoughts. But when Izzy suggested they prop his worktable chair under the doorknob as an added precaution, Benji began to thaw.

Izzy did exactly what Benji told her. She kept her voice down and even tiptoed when he sent her to the bathroom to fill the glass of water. Brooke was amazed. Izzy didn't bounce around and she didn't hee-haw. Once she whispered to Brooke, "How'm I doing?" Brooke gave her a thumbs-up sign.

Gradually Benji was won over. He got out the soap dish and let Izzy choose what to feed Lucifur from among his replenished collection of baby food hidden behind the *National Geographic*s in his bookcase. It's going to go okay, thought Brooke.

Finally Benji unlocked the door of his office. Lucifur crawled down the wall and crouched over his dinner while Benji explained to Izzy about his wing-hands. Brooke unearthed the drawing that Benji had made for her, and Izzy gaped from Lucifur to the piece of paper and back again. Every now and then Lucifur cocked a bright eye at them and clicked his tongue as if to make sure they were paying attention. Brooke watched his ears prick up, scanning the murmur of their voices.

When he was through eating, Lucifur drank some water from the tip of the eye-dropper and then crawled back up the wall. The three of them sat cross-legged on the floor, watching him.

Benji had relaid the piece of blue carpet in his office but only part of it showed. The other part was covered with newspaper. Above the newspaper, high in his favorite corner, Lucifur hung motionless, stuffed to the gills with strained beef dinner.

"What's he doing?" whispered Izzy.

"Nothing," said Benji. The glass of water with the eyedropper in it rested on the floor between his gloved hands. "He's digesting."

"How long does that take?" asked Izzy.

"Not long," Brooke said.

"Sssh," said Benji suddenly. "He's about to."

Lucifur swung slightly, as if to gain momentum, and then executed a neat half cartwheel. Now he hung from his thumbs, turned around, other end up. He looked funnier to Brooke somehow, with his feet dangling instead of his head.

"Why did he do that?" asked Izzy.

There was a faint *rat-ta-ta-tat* sound on the newspaper.

"He didn't want to dribble down his stomach," Benji told her.

"Watch!" Brooke whispered.

Lucifur was swiveling his hips from side to side as if in time to some jazz beat. A few random drops landed on the newspaper.

"He's dancing!" exclaimed Izzy.

"No," said Benji. "It's what boys do."

"Girls, too," Brooke said. "He's shaking to dry himself off. Like we do, Izzy, in the woods, when there's only poison ivy for toilet paper."

After a moment something else fell on the newspaper.

"Guano," said Benji. "It's full of nitrates." He cleared his throat. "In the Civil War they used it for making gunpowder, but I'm throwing it on Mom's garden."

Lucifur still hung by his thumbs, but

when nothing more fell, he cartwheeled back to upside down again. Then he twisted around and peered at them with an expression of such smug self-satisfaction that Izzy's upper lip rolled back and she had to cover her mouth with her hand.

"He's so proud of himself he can hardly stand it." Brooke wanted to hug him.

"Exactly like my little nephew," said Izzy, "when he's *finally* done something on the potty. He makes everyone come and admire it."

Lucifur had begun to clean himself. Benji got up, smiling a slight, secret smile, and carried the glass of water and the empty soap dish into the bathroom.

From somewhere below them, Brooke heard the steady rasp of sawing. Sam at work in the bindery. She sniffed. A sweet-sour smell of vinegar and brown sugar and spices permeated the house. Mom's pickling watermelon rinds in the kitchen, she thought. Next to her Izzy unfolded her legs and stretched. Lucifur seemed to have fallen asleep.

"You were right," Izzy said. "He's absolutely adorable. I can't believe it. When you told me about him I thought you'd gone bananas. I was actually *scared* to come. Honestly! How dumb can you be!"

"Well, sometimes he is a little scary,"

said Brooke. "When he flies. Until you get used to him."

"I thought he might go for me," Izzy said. "My neck. I thought he only drank blood. Stupid. I mean, *stupid!*"

"Everyone thinks that," said Benji. He had come out of the bathroom and was standing behind them. "Because of vampires. All people ever think of are vampires because of Dracula and comics, so whenever they see bats, they scream and make up more lies about them and put it on television. But there are hundreds of different kinds of bats, fruit bats, and fish-catching bats. And, and bats as big as eagles and bats who can see pretty well and bats who can't, and vampires are just one kind." He took a deep breath and kept on going. "They're the only kind that drinks blood, and they only live in South America and other bats don't like them either. Other bats won't even roost with them. They make them sleep in a different part of the cave. By themselves. Lucifur isn't a vampire at all." Benji had run out of breath.

"I know he isn't, Benj," said Brooke.

"He's really good," said Benji. "He eats mosquitoes and moths, and he's one of the best fliers and scientists study him and study him."

"He's neat," said Izzy. "Mousy. No, I

don't mean that. Cuter than a mouse. He's as good as a dog."

"Better than a dog," interrupted Brooke. "Smarter. Look at Delilah. You can't train her to do anything, and Lucifur has learned to eat out of a dish and come when he's called already."

"How did you teach him, Benji?" asked Izzy.

Benji shrugged. "I was lucky. Lucifur cooperated. Mostly they don't. They're wild, you know." He cleared his throat. "You want to hear something funny? The army tried to make bats into bat bombers once. They had this plan. They strapped tiny, tiny fire bombs to their chests and then they were going to air-drop them over enemy cities. The bats were supposed to chew their bombs off and start millions of fires. But you know what? This is the good part. Before the army got a chance to try it, some of the bats escaped and burned down an airplane hangar and blew up a general's jeep."

"Come off it, Benji," said Brooke.

"No. It's true." Benji looked at her side-ways, pleased.

"You're kidding," said Izzy. "What else? What else did they do?"

"Well . . ." Benji stared into his office at Lucifur. "The scientists tried another way. They thought if the bats were sleepy, they would do what the army wanted. So they put them in an animal icebox and made them very cold and then they airdropped them. But it still didn't work. It was awful." Benji stopped talking. He wiggled his loose tooth with his tongue. A smear of blood appeared on his bottom lip. He licked it off.

"What happened?" asked Brooke.

"Go on," said Izzy.

"They didn't wake up," said Benji bluntly. "They were all killed."

Brooke pictured hundreds of small black shapes falling and falling, their wings like parachutes that never opened.

"That's mean," said Izzy. "Poor little bats."

"Why did they make them cold?" Brooke asked after a moment.

"To force them to hibernate," explained Benji.

"I didn't know bats hibernated," said Brooke. "I guess I thought they migrated, like birds."

"Some do. Some don't. In the tropics, they just stay where they are."

"What about Lucifur?" asked Brooke. "The nights are getting colder already."

"You want this empty baby food jar, Izzy?" offered Benji. "For paint or something?"

"Sure. For bobby pins. The top of my bureau's a mess."

"Does Lucifur hibernate?" Brooke repeated.

"Yes, but. . . ." Benji moved away toward his worktable. "But he won't have to."

"But should he?" persisted Brooke.

"Not if I keep him warm. I won't open my windows, ever. And, and I'll insulate my office. Somehow. And it'll be better for him, he'll like it better than sleeping in a dirty, cold, crowded cave."

"Slow down, Benji. That's not the point," said Brooke. "The point is, are you going against his nature? Will it hurt him to be up all winter?"

Benji didn't answer.

"It might wear him out," Brooke went on. "Maybe he needs that rest time."

"Then he can hibernate here. With me. I'll leave my windows open all the time and wear my long underwear and my ski hat to bed."

"For Pete's sake, Benji, that's crazy! With Mom and Dad on an energy-saving binge, prowling the house for drafts. Think about it. Remember last winter when the fuel bills came in and Dad hit the roof. You'll never get away with it. And then what would happen to Lucifur? He might die, Benji."

138

"He won't die," said Benji. His eyes looked feverish. "He won't die. I won't let him."

"Maybe you could just let him go," suggested Izzy. "Before school opens."

"School?" For a moment Benji looked confused and then color flared in his face. He yanked off his gloves and marched across the room, brushing against Brooke as he passed. He threw the gloves into his office and swung the door shut. The padlock closed with a snap.

Izzy glanced at Brooke, startled. "When am I going to get to see him fly?" she asked.

Benji turned his back on them both. "Never," he said.

Chapter 13

"I queered it," said Izzy the next morning for the hundredth time. "I'm a total hick-head!"

"It wasn't you. It was me," said Brooke. "I was the one who kept bugging him about hibernation."

They sat wedged together on the Banuchis' backyard swing; occasionally Izzy dug the toe of her sneaker into the worn trough of ground beneath the swing to keep them rocking. Mr. and Mrs. Banuchi were at the hardware store. Mike was mowing the front lawn. Brooke could hear the sound of the mower revving and fading as Mike turned corners. It was a summer sound but sad, she thought, too clear and too sharp, a sound carried on autumn air.

"Have you tried talking to him?" asked Izzy.

"I couldn't at supper. And now he's barricaded the door. I knocked on it this morning and then I tried to open it, but it didn't budge. He's put the chair under the handle, I think."

"Oh, no! That was my idea. What about the bathroom door?"

"I tried that, too," said Brooke, "but something's holding it. I think he's tied it shut."

"Could you hear anything?"

Brooke shook her head.

"The keyhole?"

"Blocked up."

Izzy groaned. "How do you know he's all right in there?" she asked.

"I don't." Brooke pressed her cheek into the chain of the swing. "Sometimes it scares me. Sometimes I think . . . oh, I don't know what I think, Izzy."

"Don't worry," said Izzy. "He'll be fine."

"That's what Mom keeps saying, but I can't help it. It's more than just yesterday. It's the whole summer. He won't see anyone except Dr. Blazer. And Mom hasn't a clue. Sometimes I think he's slowly tuning out and I'm the only one who cares and now he's locked me out, too." Brooke didn't dare go on. She stood up abruptly keeping her face turned away. There was a silence. Brooke kept swallowing. Then she heard the swing creak and Izzy appeared beside her.

"Okay," said Izzy, "we've got to get in

there. That's all there is to it."

"How?"

"Think! You're the brain. Bribery. Some sort of present. What would he like? A toy, a creamy, books?"

"He's got a libraryful already."

"Candy? Fruit Loops? Bubble gum? I know, what about more baby food?"

"Baby food? No. Well, maybe. Wait a minute. You've given me an idea. Where's your phone book? I've got to check something."

There were breakfast dishes on the Banuchis' dining room table. The phone book was under the pile of newspapers at Mrs. Banuchi's place. Brooke flipped to the yellow pages in back.

"Shoot! I forgot to clear the table," Izzy said.

"P . . . PE. . . ." Brooke muttered to herself. Her fingers stopped moving. "Can I use your phone?"

Izzy nodded.

Brooke dialed in the kitchen. The rest of the breakfast dishes were in the kitchen sink. Izzy appeared in the doorway juggling a load of dirty coffee cups as Brooke hung up.

"How far would you guess South Starksboro was?" Brooke asked.

"About five miles? Why?"

"They have a pet shop, but we'll have to

hurry. I have to be home by two to sit with Benji. Get your bike. And your knapsack. I'll get mine and meet you by the cannon."

"Bike!" neighed Izzy. "We're going to bike there! Up that humungus hill! It'll kill me! Why are we going? Why do we have to? Give me one good reason!"

"Mealworms."

Brooke propped her bike against the wall of the porch.

"I don't dare get off," said Izzy. "My legs are wobbly. But I've gotta have something to drink. I'm totally dehydrated." She let her bike keel over and stumbled up the porch steps.

"You sound like Jason."

"Is he here?" Izzy mopped at her face with the sleeve of her tee shirt. "My hair's a mess. Do I look organic?"

Jason was in the front hall bending over some shopping bags. At the slam of the screen door, he straightened up and turned toward them.

"Jeez," breathed Izzy.

He was wearing his soccer uniform. Even in the dimness of the hall the bright yellow jersey was hard to miss. The sleeves were striped from the shoulder to the wrists in black and white, and below the padded black shorts, he wore yellow knee socks banded in black. His cleats had brand-new yellow laces, which he had wrapped around his insteps and tied on top. Brooke had never seen the laces before.

"How do I look?" he asked.

Izzy's lips were moving but no words came out of her mouth.

"You look like a bumblebee," said Brooke.

Jason ignored her. "Big game this afternoon," he said to Izzy. "Exhibition. You can come if you want."

"No, she can't," said Brooke.

Izzy closed her mouth. Jason picked up the shopping bags. "Come on, Mom, Dad. Brooke's back," he hollered.

Mr. and Mrs. Forbes came down the stairs. Jason held the screen door open.

"Oh, hi, Izzy," said Mrs. Forbes. "Sorry to run. Brooke, check on Benji, will you? See if you can get him to eat something."

"I've got the Gatorade and oranges," Jason said.

"It's going to be a great game," said Mr. Forbes.

"There are apples in the fruit bowl," Mrs. Forbes went on. "And ice cream in the freezer."

"Did he take his ... pill?" asked Brooke.

"Brooke!" Mr. Forbes broke in sharply. "You're holding us up. Let's get this show on the road."

"I made oatmeal cookies specially." Mrs.

Forbes fingered the top button of her shirt. "See what you can do," she said, and then they were gone.

"Is this Jason's last game?" asked Izzy.

"Who knows," said Brooke. "Get the stuff."

Izzy shrugged out of her knapsack and untied the flap. She held up a plastic container. "Mealworms are revolting," she said. "Like shiny brown grubs with little legs in front. Should we gift wrap them?"

"No. I'll slip a note under his door."

His door was just an ordinary door but it seemed impenetrable, thought Brooke a few minutes later.

"Benji," she called. She didn't bother to knock. "Listen, Benji, I'm slipping a note under the door." There was no answer. "Okay?"

"Leave a corner showing," whispered Izzy crouching beside her, "so we can tell."

Brooke pressed her ear against the door. "He's coming." The white triangle of paper slid from view.

"He took it," whispered Izzy. Brooke let out her breath.

They were still on their knees when Benji opened the door and looked down at them. "Let me see them," he said.

Brooke got to her feet, feeling silly, and handed him the container.

"Gee, thanks. I wondered what they

looked like." He opened the container and sniffed. "Where did you get them?"

"We biked for hours. To this pet shop," Izzy told him.

"They're really hard to find, Benj," added Brooke. "They have to fly them in from California."

Benji had crossed the room to the window and was holding the container up to the sunlight. In profile his body seemed too narrow, as if there were nothing inside the outline of his sweat shirt and jeans. Maybe it was the light playing tricks, Brooke thought.

"Mom's made cookies," she said to him. "Do you want some?"

"No. I'm not hungry. Can you get more of these mealworms?"

"Sure, and they're not that expensive. Only seventy-five cents a portion."

The blue comforter from Benji's bed draped over the top of his office and hung down the side. Oh, thought Brooke, for Lucifur.

"I've got to tell Noah," said Benji.

"Who?" asked Izzy.

"Dr. Blazer. Benji likes him," said Brooke between her teeth. "I told you. They're friends."

Izzy rolled her eyes.

"Lucifur's going to love these things," said Benji, "but I'm not going to let him have them yet. Nope. Gotta fly first. Gotta get some exercise. He's getting spoiled and lazy and out of practice."

He sounded all right, and his chair was drawn up to his worktable, exactly where it should be. For a moment Brooke wondered whether she'd been exaggerating things, but then she noticed a length of clothesline hanging from his bathroom doorknob.

"Where's Mom and Dad?" Benji asked.

"At Jason's soccer game. He invited me, too," said Izzy.

"Good," said Benji. He unlocked his office. Lucifur hung in the corner, curled like a dried autumn leaf. "Open the bathroom door, Brooke," Benji said.

He set the mealworms down next to his typewriter and picked up his gloves. He put them on, talking to Lucifur all the time. "Wake up, wake up, little bat. Time to fly. If you're good, I've got a treat for you." Lucifur didn't budge. Brooke watched Benji reach up and pluck him off his perch. Lucifur blinked at her from the nest of Benji's fingers.

"Sit down, Izzy," advised Brooke. The door to Benji's room was still open. Brooke shut it tight. They'd almost forgotten about it.

"Sleepy bat," said Benji. Lucifur yawned. Benji planted his feet and launched him into the air. Lucifur unfurled his wings, but he didn't take off. Instead he descended to the worktable in a long, slow glide.

"Oh, no," said Benji. "Stop pretending. You can fly in the daytime if you have to. I know you can. You're just goofing off." He tossed Lucifur up again. This time Lucifur flew.

Izzy put her arms over her hair but she didn't scream.

"Doesn't he like to go into the bathroom anymore?" asked Brooke after a while. "He keeps swerving away as if the door was closed."

"I knew it. He's getting too used to this room," said Benji. "That door's been closed the last couple of times, so he figures it still is. He's not listening for echoes."

"Echoes?" asked Izzy. "Echoes of what?"

"Of his own voice," Benji explained. "Lucifur can't see too well, so he flies by sound. He shrieks when he flies. Short shrieks, bleep . . . bleep . . . bleep. . . . Fifty times a second. The bleeps bounce off everything in his way, sending echoes back, and he listens for them all the time. The echoes tell him where things are, like doors or lamps or bugs. They make a kind of picture to fly by." Benji coughed. "It's called echolocation. But Lucifur isn't bothering to do it so much. He's turned it down."

"Make him turn it up again," said Brooke. "All he's doing is winging it, back and forth, back and forth. It's boring and I promised Izzy."

"That's okay," said Izzy. She had lowered her arms, but her chin was still scrunched down as far it it would go into the collar of her shirt. "Really. I was just wondering, does he fly any lower?"

"Hey," said Benji abruptly. "I'm going to try something." He disappeared into the bathroom. Brooke and Izzy scuttled after him. Benji took the glass and eyedropper out of the medicine cabinet and filled the glass with water. Then he opened the other door, crossed Brooke's room, and sat down with his back against the wall. Brooke and Izzy sat down beside him, but he seemed to have forgotten they were there. His eyes were riveted on the bathroom doorways. Without looking down, he clinked on the glass with the eyedropper.

Lucifur flashed once across the far opening, reappeared, and hovered for an instant. Benji clinked again. Louder. Lucifur streaked through the bathroom and into Brooke's room. He skimmed along the wall just above Brooke's head. Benji put the glass down.

"He's turned on again," he whispered. "Echolocating."

Shafts of late afternoon sunlight invaded the room. Lucifur darted through the suspended dust motes, and the shimmering particles swirled in his wake. He scudded across the top of Brooke's bureau, whirred around the lampshade, and then, without hesitating, shot through the slats of the ladder-back rocking chair.

"Jeez," gasped Izzy. "He's like those crazy stunt pilots who fly under bridges!"

"If Noah had seen that, he would have picked him for the experiment. For sure," said Benji. "I wish . . . I wish things were . . . different." His voice faded and his head tilted back. He stared at the ceiling.

Experiment, thought Brooke. He'd mentioned one that other night in the kitchen, but she'd yelled at him and he'd clammed up.

"Benj?" she said, keeping her voice low and cajoling. "What experiment, Benj?"

"The one with the wires and the bells that Noah's built," answered Benji. "In his barn. The one he's going to do when he gets back from Washington. I'm in charge of feeding. To keep them flying through the grids."

"What grids, Benj?"

"The wire ones with bells hanging on them. Noah's going to make the bats fly through them in the night blindfolded to test their echolocation. To find out if they can do it without touching the wires. If they touch a wire, we'll know, you see, 'cause a bell will ring and Noah will mark it down as a 'miss.' And he's going to take pictures of everything with this new camera that can work in the dark."

Lucifur swooped in and out of Brooke's sight.

"Noah says," Benji went on as if he were talking to himself, "that they fly with their mouths wide open and the pictures will show it. They're yelling all the time at the top of their lungs, but it's too high for us to hear. It's ultrasonic. If the experiment works one hundred percent, we won't hear the bells either. The only thing we'll hear is silence."

Chapter 14

Brooke and Izzy were almost finished with the scraping. It was amazing. They'd done a side and a half in one day. Actually, the garage looked worse than before, Brooke decided, scarred with patches of bare wood as if it were infected with some dreadful spreading fungus, but that would get better as soon as they could begin on the first coat. Everything was better. She and Izzy . . . Benji. He seemed fine again, full of purpose and funny ideas. She smiled at the garage wall, feeling happy. Even Delilah was off hassling someone else for once. They hadn't laid eyes on her all day. And Brooke's shoulders didn't ache. I'm not even tired, she thought, and I should be exhausted considering that Sam woke the whole house at dawn with his sawing and hammering in the bindery. Only Lucifur had slept through it.

"I guess Dr. Blazer's just your normal

psycho scientist," said Izzy, "but if I ever so much as see him touch a meat cleaver, I'll break the three-minute mile."

Brooke stopped scraping and peered down at her. "I still wonder what his connection is with all those government places. Remember his mail?" The Bomb Data Center was the place she remembered. "Maybe I'll find out. Benji's going to ask him whether I can come to the experiment. It might make a great project for science this year. Want to do it with me?"

"Well," said Izzy. "I'll do it if you'll do it. Hey, I bet nobody else has ever done bats. We'd get an A plus just for thinking the idea up."

"I'll find out if you can come, too."

"Okay," said Izzy. "That takes care of science. I'm going to do everything differently at school this year. I'm throwing out my old stuff. Starting fresh. I've already bought a new three-ring binder, two sets of dividers, so that math doesn't run into French; a pencil case that attaches, with everything I need in it: ruler, protractor, and a cute little pencil sharpener. And a new assignment book, a really good one, that will force me to be organized. Every night I'll fold the page over so I'll know when I've done all my homework. I think that's the secret to making honor roll."

"You said the exact same thing last

year," said Brooke. She stood midway on the ladder working on the last rough section near the garage door.

"But this year is different," said Izzy. "It's high school. Besides, I'm going to make a daily schedule and scotchtape it to my mirror and I'm going to lay out my clothes the night before, even down to Kotex and Tampax when I have to. Don't look at me like that. Wait and see. I'm going to be a changed person."

"I like it when you open your binder and everything falls out. It makes me feel good."

"Never, never again," said Izzy. "I bought three boxes of those hole reinforcements. I love all this getting ready. It's the best part. The worst part is going back."

"I know. That's what I said to Benji this morning, but he's got it solved. He says he's not going."

"Not going back to school! Who says?"

"He does. Anyway, that's what he told me. He says he's going to get Mom to tutor him. I felt like laughing, but I didn't dare. He seemed so positive and I didn't know where to begin to tell him."

"Does your mom know?"

"Of course not. Can you see her boning up on new math? And Eskimos? But Benji's completely serious. Talk about reorganizing! He's cleaning out his room, piling junk in the hall. And wrapping things up in wads of toilet paper. Presents, he says."

"Like what?"

"I'll show you." Brooke climbed down the ladder. "One's for you anyway."

"We've done enough," said Izzy.

They sat on the grass in the shade of the garage. Brooke dug in her pockets and pulled out two wadded white packages.

"It's like one of those party surprise balls," said Izzy, unrolling yards and yards of toilet paper. "It's a . . . it's a dinosaur! And it's painted so realistically. It's even got food hanging out of its mouth."

Brooke had finished unraveling hers. "Mine, too. Dried pigweed."

"They're wonderful. So . . . ecological. I'm going to use mine to hold my books open when I'm taking notes."

They *were* wonderful, thought Brooke; better than the plastic kind they sold in the five-and-ten. Bigger, more imaginative, with such authentic details, plates and knobs and triangular spines. She turned her ankylosaur over in her hands. Something about it seemed familiar. A thought niggled at the back of her mind and then faded away.

"Let's go thank him," said Izzy. "You put the stuff back. I'll sign out. I want to see Lucifur. Shoot, will he be awake this early? It's only three-thirty."

"I don't know," said Brooke. She rested the ladder horizontally against the garage wall. "But you'd have to be dead to sleep through the racket Sam's making."

"Talk about dead," said Izzy a moment later. "I don't think those azaleas are going to make it." The clump of bushes in the middle of Mrs. Gibson's lawn looked beleaguered, as if they were making a last stand. Delilah had been digging around them and some of the branches were chewed and broken off. Only a few leaves and shriveled blossoms clung to the bare twigs. "Mrs. Gibson never should have tried planting them in the middle of summer. Any idiot could have told her that."

"Maybe your father can save them," said Brooke.

"Forget it," said Izzy. "I'm much more interested in seeing that zingbat."

Brooke slowed. "Wait a minute. What's that? Look. There. In the middle of the road. Up ahead. At the end of Dr. Blazer's driveway."

Izzy squinted. "It's somebody's old bathrobe. Blazer's probably."

Brooke was only half listening. "No. It's not flat enough. And it's furry. And — oh, Izzy!" She started to run and stopped. "Oh, no. It's Delilah!"

Izzy came up right behind her and stuck there, close and touching. "She's been run over. Do you think she's dead?" she whispered.

Brooke was hardly breathing. She wanted somebody else to find out, to deal with it. She couldn't move.

"No. Look. She's trying to lift her head," Brooke said. Now she couldn't just stand there anymore.

"Don't go near her. She might be bloody. Mashed. Her guts hanging out. Don't, Brooke. Wait!" Izzy was yelling after her.

But there was no blood that Brooke could see. None on the road, none matting Delilah's fur, none at the corners of her mouth. Brooke crouched down. "Good girl. It's all right. Good girl, good girl. It's all right," she repeated over and over, a mindless litany to calm herself.

Delilah raised her head in response and swung it blindly from side to side. She whimpered deep in her throat.

"She hurts," said Brooke, "but I can't see where."

"Maybe it's internal hemorrhaging," said Izzy. "A hit and run?"

Delilah was trying to get up. "Lie still," said Brooke. She reached out a tentative hand. "You've got to lie still." But Delilah heaved her chest off the ground and struggled to straighten her front legs.

They trembled violently with the effort. She lurched forward and her hindquarters dragged a few inches. The back part of her seems dead already, thought Brooke. She heard the rasp of claws on the pavement. Then the dog's forelegs buckled and she collapsed onto her side. A shudder ran the length of her body and she stiffened and lay still.

Help, thought Brooke. She looked wildly around. There was no van in Dr. Blazer's driveway. The doors of his barn were closed and the shades were pulled on the front windows of his house.

"Go! Get Mom!" she said to Izzy. "Quick! Run!"

Izzy fled.

I should get out of the road, thought Brooke, before I'm run over, too. She had never seen anything die before and she didn't want to see it now. But she stayed where she was.

Delilah was still breathing. Brooke stroked her ears and back and watched the heaving of the dog's stomach as if stroking and watching were the key to each breath. Under her fingers the fur was soft and silky, rippled with light, as if it had just been washed and brushed and buffed to a high sheen. Poor Mrs. Gibson. Brooke hadn't noticed before how beautiful Delilah was. Her hand grew numb from patting. Don't die, Delilah, she thought. Please don't die. In the distance she could hear the sound of a hammer.

The hammering stopped. The screen door slammed and then slammed again. Izzy ran toward her leading Sam and Mrs. Forbes.

"Hang it!" breathed Sam. "Lemme have a look."

Brooke stood up and stepped back. Her knees were trembling. "I think her rear end's paralyzed," she said.

"A car must have hit her," Izzy said.

"Creep," said Sam.

"Maybe we shouldn't move. . . ." Mrs. Forbes began, but Sam had already gathered Delilah into his arms and was struggling to his feet. "Lotta dog," he grunted. "I'll take her in the truck. Somebody get a blanket."

"There's one in the station wagon," Brooke offered. Her mother nodded.

"You did just right, young lady," said Sam. Delilah whimpered and was racked with another spasm. Sam hung on until it was over and then hefted her to get a firmer grip.

Benji was standing on the front lawn. "Is she dead?" he asked.

"Not yet," Brooke told him. She scrambled into the station wagon and pulled the old army blanket out of the back.

Izzy and Mrs. Forbes unhooked the tail-gate of Sam's truck.

"Spread it out," Sam said to Brooke. He was panting. He lowered Delilah gently and folded the edges of the blanket around her.

"Someone's got to ride in back with her," he said.

"I'll go," said Mrs. Forbes. "Oh gosh, I can't. I forgot. It's awards day at Jason's camp and a soccer banquet after. At the field. I'm meeting Allen there. I can't not go. And where's Dotty? Brooke, you've got to keep calling her house."

"Okay, Izzy. In you go," said Sam.

"Oh, Sam," Mrs. Forbes drew her breath through her teeth. "Do you think she can handle that?"

"She'll do fine," said Sam.

He gave Izzy a boost up. The he closed and latched the tailgate and rattled it to make sure it was secure. "Knock on the window if you need me." He had the engine running and the truck in reverse before he closed the door of the cab.

"Brooke. There's a casserole for you and Benji all made on the kitchen table," called Mrs. Forbes, braking the station wagon halfway out of the driveway. "Three hundred and fifty degrees." She paused. "I'm sorry to leave you with all this. Will you be all right?"

A moment later Brooke and Benji were alone. The sounds of the motors faded into silence.

"Yell if Mrs. Gibson goes by," Brooke said.

"Yell what?" asked Benji. "I don't know what happened."

"I'll be back in a sec, as soon as I've tried to phone her."

Listening to the ringing at the other end, Brooke trailed the telephone cord into the kitchen to check the clock. She was surprised to find it was only five minutes to four.

Chapter 15

Benji had assumed a lookout position on the top step of the porch and was sitting, chin in hands, staring at the road.

"A delivery truck and old Miss Griggs in her Jeep. That's it so far," he reported when Brooke returned. She handed him an apple.

"Tell," he said.

So she went back over it all again, from the first sight of Delilah crumpled in the road to when Sam had come to lift and carry her to his truck. "It was really horrible. And scary," she said.

"Scary," agreed Benji in a low voice.

Seeing him nod and hearing the word from someone else made Brooke feel better.

"I wonder if she knows what's happening? If she's scared, too?" Benji went on.

"Who?" asked Brooke. "Mrs. Gibson?"

"No. Delilah. Do you think she's going to die?"

"I don't know, Benj. I hope not."

"I think she is," said Benji. "I wonder if dying makes dogs sad. Like it does people."

Brooke didn't answer.

"I'll ask Noah," said Benji. "When he gets back."

"What's the point in that? He wasn't even there."

"Doesn't matter," said Benji. "He'll know."

"Stay here," said Brooke. "I'm going to try Mrs. Gibson again."

This time she counted seven rings before she hung up. It was quarter past four. By five forty-five she had dialed Mrs. Gibson's number eight more times, they had fed Lucifur, and she had put the casserole in the oven.

"What's keeping everyone? I wish I'd gone with Izzy."

"Sssh," said Benji. "There's a truck coming." He listened. "It's Sam's. I heard the clutch-bang."

Izzy was in the cab next to Sam. Sam pulled up on the far side of Ashpotag and leaned across to open Izzy's door.

"How's Delilah?" Brooke asked, stepping onto the running board.

"Absolutely awful," said Izzy. "She kept having these horrendous spasms all the way there. Her eyes would roll up and her legs would shake and then she'd go all rigid.

And she threw up, on the blanket and on me, too. Look," she said, coming around the front of the truck. "I'm covered with vomit."

Benji stood very still on the road below Brooke. He looked up at Sam's pumpkin face in the window of the cab.

"What did the vet say?" Benji asked.

"Didn't say much," said Sam. "Didn't know much, is my guess. Totally bamboozled by the whole thing. But he couldn't find any broken bones. What did I tell you? It wasn't a car."

"Did he give her a pill?" Benji persisted.

"Nope. A needle. Knocked her out for the time being." The motor of the truck was still running. Sam shifted gears.

"Aren't you staying?" asked Brooke. She was still on the running board. "Mom's not back and I haven't reached Mrs. Gibson yet. But she's got to be home any minute." There was a cowlick in Sam's right eyebrow and Brooke stared at it. "I could make you a cup of coffee and then you could tell her. Please, Sam."

Sam considered. "I was going to take the garbage to the dump, but I guess it could wait." He turned off the ignition. Brooke loosened her hold on the door of the cab. "But I'll have to let the missus know, and make that a diet soda instead. My stomach's spreading around to the back."

"Brooke," said Benji suddenly. "She's here." He pointed.

Mrs. Gibson's car had pulled up behind the truck. Her head was sticking out of the window.

"What are you all doing in the middle of the road? Lucky I don't drive like a maniac or I'd have run you over for sure."

Sam lumbered down from the cab. Brooke and Izzy and Benji were shielded by his bulk.

"You look like death warmed over," Mrs. Gibson went on. "What is this, Sam? Why are you looking at me like that?"

"Evenin', Dotty," said Sam. "Brooke here's just offered some soda and I thought I'd take her up on it. Why don't you come on in?"

"Well . . . I should get home and say hello to Delilah. She's been alone all day, but I guess a few minutes more won't hurt." Brooke heard Benji clear his throat. Mrs. Gibson got out of her car, repinning her bun with both hands. "I could use a cup of coffee after the day I've had." She arched her back and stretched. "And I've got something for you, girls. The paint. At last. I stopped at the hardware and that nice brother of yours, Izzy, helped me load it into the back of my car. It's a lovely red. Wait 'til you see it. I hope you finished the scraping, dears." She smiled at Brooke's and Izzy's nods. "My, my, Benji, talk about color. You could use some yourself. You look like a mushroom."

Sam led her across the road.

Brooke skirted them with Benji in tow. "I'll go put the kettle on."

"I'll help," said Izzy.

Just as they reached the porch, they heard a gasp and then a wail. Brooke glanced around. Mrs. Gibson was staring up at Sam and he was patting her shoulder.

"He's told her. Don't watch. Keep going," advised Izzy.

The kettle was on, Benji had set a mug and spoon on the table, and Izzy was getting down the instant coffee, when Sam half supported Mrs. Gibson into the kitchen. Brooke held an empty glass in her hand.

"Sam, we don't have any diet soda. I could give you orange juice."

"Got a cold beer? I think I'd rather have that," said Sam, pulling out a chair for Mrs. Gibson. "Do you know where your Dad keeps the brandy?"

"I do," said Benji. "I'll get it."

Brooke poured hot water into the mug. "And here's sugar and cream," she said.

"I can't believe it. I just can't believe it." Mrs. Gibson's hands fluttered over the dishes. She picked up the spoon, stirred her coffee, and then left the spoon standing upright in the mug. "She was fine this morning. Wasn't she, girls? You must have seen her." Mrs. Gibson looked at each of them beseechingly. Brooke and Izzy stood silently side by side, their backs against the kitchen sink. Benji trotted in from the hall and put the bottle of brandy by Sam's elbow. Sam uncorked it with one pull.

"Have a splash of this, Dotty. In your coffee," he said.

"Are you crazy, Sam!" Mrs. Gibson clapped a hand over the top of her mug. "I can't sit here drinking. I've got to go. I've got to drive to the vet's." She took her hand away and fumbled in her bag. Cigarettes, thought Brooke, and brought a saucer.

"Now, hold your horses, Dotty. No point going off half-cocked." Sam patted his pockets and came up with a book of matches. "Here." He lit one and leaned toward her. Mrs. Gibson's cigarette trembled. "The dog isn't even there."

"Not there!" wailed Mrs. Gibson. "What do you mean?"

"I mean she's not there and neither is the vet," Sam continued. "They're on their way to Burlington to the Animal Medical Center so's they can run some tests."

"Tests! What kind of tests?"

Sam shook his head. He took a long swallow from his glass of beer and then another. He wiped his upper lip with the back of his hand and looked at Brooke. "Get me a little glass, a shot glass, would you?"

"I'll get it," said Benji.

"Tell me the truth, Sam," said Mrs. Gibson. "Is she dying? Don't try to spare me. I'm one of those people who have to know."

"Well, she's sick. Real sick. That's for sure," said Sam. There was a moan from Mrs. Gibson.

Benji came back, bearing the miniature glass. Sam took it out of his hand. He filled the glass with brandy and tossed the drink to the back of his throat. Brooke watched him swallow. "Chaser," he muttered to himself.

"I still bet she was run over," said Izzy. "She was lying right in the middle of the road, remember?"

Mrs. Gibson took another cigarette and Sam lit it for her. Brooke reached over and put out the one still burning in the ashtray.

"She wasn't bleeding at all, Mrs. Gibson," she said, "and she never stopped breathing."

"The vet couldn't put his finger on it, but he was sure it wasn't a car," said Sam. "He wouldn't say more than that. Not until the tests are done. So we'll have to wait and see. Maybe she'll come out of it on her own. She's got a real strong constitution."

Benji slipped out of the kitchen. Brooke heard his footsteps on the stairs.

"I've got to get home," said Mrs. Gibson. "Throw a few things in a bag. I'm going to Burlington. My ex-sister-in-law lives there. I'll stay with her. Oh, mercy! I'm not thinking straight. We're not speaking. I'll stay in a motel."

"Calm down. Finish your coffee first," said Sam.

"Izzy and I can unload the paint from your car," offered Brooke.

"And we'll work like dogs while you're gone," added Izzy. "Oh, jeez. I mean hard, really hard."

Brooke heard Benji's cough. He was back, standing in the doorway, mouthing something at her. What was wrong with him? thought Brooke, annoyed.

"I've always had a dog in the house," said Mrs. Gibson. She sniffed twice.

Brooke read Benji's lips. *Lucifer.* But there was more she didn't catch. *What?* she mouthed back.

He's gone. Benji exaggerated the enunciation of each word.

"She's always slept on my bed." Mrs. Gibson blew her nose. "I've never been in that house alone."

Where? mouthed Brooke.

Benji shrugged his shoulders.

"I don't know what I'm going to do if —
if — oh, I'm so distraught!" Mrs. Gibson
stirred her coffee. Then she tapped the
spoon against the rim of the mug before
putting it down on the table.

Lucifur swooped through the kitchen
door over Benji's head.

Chapter 16

For a moment Benji didn't see him. Nobody saw him but Brooke. Mrs. Gibson took a sip of coffee and mashed out her cigarette in the saucer. Holding his beer bottle upside down, Sam watched the last drops fall into his glass. Izzy scratched at a hard-to-reach place between her shoulder blades. Her head was bent.

Then Brooke saw Benji look up and smile.

Lucifur winged across the kitchen, nosed up, banked, and sailed back. He turned and made another pass.

Keep going, prayed Brooke, as he wafted back toward the door. Go, go. The incessant flutter of his wings seemed to fill the room. Couldn't they hear it?

Lucifur banked again over Benji's head.

Benji stood motionless. The smile was gone from his face. He's realized, thought Brooke. Lucifur's not lost, but all hell's about to break loose. I've got to do something. Quick. Lure him out before the others see him. Distract them. She clutched for an idea, a plan, but came up with nothing. Instead she just stood there like an idiot, as frozen as Benji, waiting for the first scream.

It came from Mrs. Gibson. A half squeal, half screech. Sam belched and looked at her, perplexed. "What the . . . ?"

"There's a bat! A bat!" she screamed.

"Bat? Where?" Sam was on his feet. Lucifur sailed sedately back and forth, like a pendulum.

"Get me a newspaper! Or a broom!" bellowed Sam. "A broom!"

"No! Don't!" cried Benji.

Mrs. Gibson pointed. "The closet. Next to the icebox!" She covered her head with her purse. Lucifur did a flyby above the kitchen table. Izzy ducked.

"Don't! Don't! He's good!" Benji blocked the front of the broom closet. "No, Sam. Please," he sobbed. But Sam flung the door open, knocking him aside. Brooke was galvanized into action.

Sam turned, armed with the broom, and flailed at Lucifur.

"Wait!" yelled Brooke, trying to intercept him. "You're wrong! Stop!" The broom whistled past her head. She grabbed for Sam's arm, but he shook her off.

"Leggo! I almost had him!" The broom connected with the kitchen light. It swung wildly. Brooke scraped the hair out of her eyes and leapt at Sam again. Benji tugged at Sam's belt from behind.

"Get him! Get him!" cried Mrs. Gibson.

Sam was trying. He took a tremendous swing. Lucifur yawed out of the way. The momentum of the miss swung Sam into a corkscrew like a batter striking out. Only Brooke was hanging on to him now. Benji had let go. "Help me," Brooke called to Izzy.

Clink, clink, clink. And then again, loud and sharp. *Clink, clink, clink.* Benji stood by the kitchen table, following Lucifur's flight with his whole body and tapping Mrs. Gibson's mug with the spoon. Calling Lucifur in.

Lucifur didn't waste an instant. He leveled off and flip-landed on Benji's shoulder.

"There, Sam. There!" Mrs. Gibson shouted. "Now's your chance!" Lucifur had had enough. He hitched down Benji's front as fast as he could and snuggled inside the open collar of his shirt.

"Oh, mercy! It's going to bite him! Do something, Sam!" yelled Mrs. Gibson.

Benji dropped the mug and spoon. Coffee splattered his bluejeans, and the mug bounced on the linoleum and rolled under the kitchen table. Brooke caught a glimpse of Izzy's horrified face.

Benji's hands were up to cover and protect Lucifur. Sam raised the broom above his shoulder to strike.

"No," squealed Izzy.

Benji! He's going to hit Benji, thought Brooke. She grabbed the bristle end from behind and hung on. "Not Benji," she snarled. The bristles crackled between her fingers.

Sam jerked the broom out of her hands and raised it higher.

"Don't!" Brooke gave one last desperate wail.

The broom stopped in midair. For a moment Brooke thought it was because of her, that Sam had finally heard and understood. But Sam wasn't listening to anyone. He was staring at Benji. Benji stared back, but his eyes were blank and unseeing. A long, drawn-out moan came from somewhere inside him. His eyeballs rolled up, turning him into someone Brooke didn't recognize.

"I never touched him." Sam lowered the broom. "I never touched him," he repeated. "As God is my witness."

But Benji began to sway and his eyelids fluttered closed. Then he went down.

Chapter 17

Was he breathing? Brooke couldn't tell. He lay on his back under the blue comforter she had snatched off the top of his office. It seemed hours ago. His eyes were closed and his face was white even against the whiteness of the pillow. She bent farther over his bed, wishing she hadn't covered him up. It made it harder to tell. Even with her face almost touching his she couldn't feel any breath. Please, Benji, please, she prayed. Do something! Breathe, snore, move. She was scared to touch him.

Then she noticed his lower lip. It bulged and flattened, in and out, in and out. She drew back with a sigh of relief. It's that old tooth. He's fiddling with that tooth.

Benji coughed. His eyelids trembled. His eyes opened and shut. He swallowed. "Where's Lucifur?" Brooke could barely hear him.

She sat down carefully on the edge of

his bed. "In his box, asleep. I told you before." Benji frowned as if he were figuring a math problem. He can't remember, he's forgotten already, thought Brooke, feeling a new stab of fear in the pit of her stomach.

The index finger on her right hand throbbed and she pressed her hand between her knees to stifle the pain and to keep from seeing the deep, red indents Benji's teeth had made when he bit her.

"I fed him," she told him again, "the rest of the mealworms and tapioca. Remember? He wasn't hurt at all and nobody guessed who he was. He's fine. Don't worry."

Benji's eyes opened again. "Was he thirsty?" Each word seemed an effort and he squinted as if seeing hurt his eyes.

Brooke nodded. Why hadn't the doctor called back? Her fingernails dug into her leg. Maybe there was something she should be doing for him. Something vital. It was almost pitch black outside his windows.

"Want me to turn off the light?" she asked him. "Or should I leave it on?"

Benji closed his eyes without answering. Somewhere downstairs a cricket chirruped against the silence of the house.

Brooke eased herself off his bed and switched off the lamp on his worktable. The light from the hall coming in through the open door was enough to see by. She moved back across his room. The door of his office was latched and the padlock hung from the metal loop, but it wasn't locked. She had meant to lock it after putting Lucifur away, but, at the last moment, she had changed her mind. He could be locked in there forever. Only Benji knew the combination. Only Benji could open it.

"Do you want something to drink?" she asked him.

"I'm too tired." He sounded exhausted. She watched him turn his head away as if that were all he could manage.

Still, Brooke hung around the edge of his bed. "I called the doctor," she said after a moment, "and left a message with his answering service. He's going to call me back. And Mom and Dad and Jason will be home soon. Okay?"

His eyes were shut. He was asleep. Should he be? Should she let him go or try to keep him awake? If he dies. . . . She sucked on her bitten finger to ease the pulsing ache. If he dies, then what do I do?

"I'm going to try the doctor again," she told him, as though saying it aloud proved that he could hear her. "I'll be right back."

Downstairs she felt for the light switches in the dark. The porch and the front hall flared with light. What time was it? Where were they? Why weren't they home? In the living room she swiped at the wall switch and yanked the chains on the lamps one after another. She left the room ablaze behind her. How long could a stupid soccer banquet take?

The phone rang like a fire alarm. Her heart jumped.

"Brooke?"

"Oh, I thought you were the doctor."

Izzy was whispering. "How's Benji?"

"Sleeping."

"You sound awful. Want me to come back over?"

Brooke shook her head.

"Brooke, are you okay?"

"Fine." No, not fine. But it was the easiest word to use. He's not. I'm not. Nothing is.

"Look, Brooke, please. Let me tell my mom. Okay?"

Not yet, thought Brooke. I can hang in a little longer. "No. Don't. I'm fine. Really." No talking about it, Mom had said. Not even with Izzy. "Mom and Dad will be home soon."

"Okay, but I had to tell Mrs. Gibson. Something. To get rid of her." Izzy sounded apologetic. "I sort of told her he did it all the time. Had these little whatevers when something scared him. I convinced her it was nothing serious, not like Delilah. I hope it was all right to say that? Anyway, it worked," she went on. "But she's going to call you later, after she's talked to the vet. From the motel."

"What about Sam?"

"I think he panicked. He muttered something and then he just took off. Did he come back?"

"No," Brooke said. "Listen, I ought to hang up. The doctor's probably trying to reach me."

"I'll call you later or you can call me anytime. I'm going to be up for hours, but I'm not doing anything. Just sticking reinforcements on about a million holes. Okay?"

The phone sat black and dead on the hall table. Brooke waited a moment and then dialed the number she had scribbled on the cover of the phone book. A woman's voice answered, the same one as before. Brooke couldn't go through it all again. An emergency? This time Brooke said yes. The doctor would call as soon as possible. She hung up.

Sucking on her finger, she went into the kitchen and snapped on the switches. The room seemed frozen in the fluorescent light, like a place surprised by burglars. Only clues were left: the dirty glasses on the kitchen table, Sam's beer bottle, the saucer full of half-smoked cigarettes, the chairs pushed back, brown coffee splattered like dried blood on the cabinet doors, and the mug on its side on the linoleum floor. Brooke stepped over the broom. She turned off the oven and then closed and latched the windows above the sink and locked the back door.

Moving methodically, she toured the rest of the downstairs, banishing darkness. In the dining room, she turned the rheostat up as far as it would go, and then, in the bindery, she turned on everything, even the high-intensity lamp her mother used for precision tooling. The neat arrangement of the tools on their pegboard infuriated her. All in order. Each in its place. Her mother's tools were there, but where was she? What did she care? "*Stop badgering me. He's fine. How many times do I have to tell you?*"

Brooke wanted to snatch an awl or a chisel off the board and gouge the smooth, sanded surface of the new shelf. She wanted to carve words. LIAR. LIAR. Rotten liar! Come home! At least come home.

She thought she heard a noise from upstairs. Brooke ran back through the rooms. The house was lit up like a carnival. Outside Benji's room she paused to slow the beating of her heart and then tiptoed in. He lay exactly as she left him. Motionless.

She checked him again and then stood uncertainly in the middle of his room. There was nothing more she could do. Nowhere to go. Finally she settled on the stairs, a few steps up from the landing. From there, she could listen for Benji, get to the phone quickly, and keep watch on the front door.

She waited, wanting to go to bed. Her finger killed her. Tears dammed her throat. She was still sitting there when her parents came home.

Chapter 18

"What are all the lights doing on?" Mr. Forbes asked. "We could see the house from a mile away." His arm was around Jason's shoulders.

"Brooke?" Mrs. Forbes peered up the stairs.

Brooke glared down through the bars of the banister. Now that they were finally home, she wanted to kill them.

"It's a hero's welcome. Right, son?" Mr. Forbes smiled at Jason.

"Right, Dad," said Jason. "Look, Brooke. I won the MVP trophy. They didn't give it until the very end. I had to sweat out the whole banquet." He was brandishing something. "It weighs a ton."

Brooke crouched, tense and silent, unable to focus on anything except a choking rage and the pain of her swollen finger.

"Brooke?" her mother said again. "What's wrong?"

"Benji!" Brooke packed everything into the word, but it wasn't enough. Her father was still grinning like an idiot.

"What? What do you mean?" Her mother just stood there.

"He's dying," said Brooke. "Dying! And you didn't come! You didn't come!"

Her parents were suddenly in motion. Her mother raced past her. Her father took the stairs three at a time. I should go up, too, thought Brooke, go with them, but she felt nailed to the stair.

Jason stood alone in the front hall, gaping at her; the trophy hung like a dead weight from the end of his arm. Brooke closed her eyes. She pressed her head against the banister and waited.

After a time, she felt someone sit down next to her and place a hand on her knee. "It's all right, sweetheart." It was her mother. "It's all right." Brooke twisted around. "Dad's just helping him into his pajamas. He's fine."

Above them a door closed.

"False alarm," announced Mr. Forbes from the top of the stairs. "Everything's under control. All he needs is a good night's sleep. Jason, turn off some of those lights, will you? It's a waste of electricity."

"You see, you just overreacted. That's all." Her mother patted Brooke's knee, three reassuring little pats.

Brooke recoiled, jerking her leg away. What were they doing, what were they trying to pull? They were acting as if nothing had happened, as if she had imagined the whole thing. They were acting as if she had made it all up. That was it, she thought suddenly. That was it. She stood up, feeling stiffness in her knees, and backed away from both of them, down to the landing. That was it. They were acting.

No. She put more distance between them. No. She wouldn't be sucked in anymore. "I don't believe you," she said. "You weren't here. You don't know what it was like. He is *not* fine." The words grated in her throat. "It was horrible. He had no eyes and then he went all stiff and then he fell down and he was twitching and jerking, and he couldn't breathe. It went on and on. He was choking. I thought he would suffocate, so I tried to open his mouth but he bit me. See!" She held up her finger. "He really bit me!"

"Oh, sweetheart. Let me have a look at it," said her mother.

"No!" Brooke snatched her hand away. "I've got to put ice on it."

But they followed her down the stairs and into the kitchen. Brooke slammed the freezer shut and carried the ice tray to the sink.

Jason came through the door. He put

his trophy down with a thump in the middle of the kitchen table. Mr. Forbes frowned at the bottles and overflowing ashtray. "Who's been into my good brandy?" he asked.

Brooke ignored the question. "Right there." She pointed. "Right where you're standing. That's where he fell and it wasn't any little faint either." She smashed the tray of ice cubes against the side of the sink.

"Hey, take it easy," said her father. "Here, I'll do that." He reached for the ice tray. Brooke dropped it into the sink and stepped back, wrapping her arms across her chest.

"And he went in his pants. Both. In front of everyone." She stared at Jason's trophy. "And I know they saw it. They could smell it!"

There was a toneless sigh from her mother, like the blowing out of candles.

Her father's head swung around. The ice cubes rattled unnoticed into a bowl. "Who's they? Who are you talking about?"

"Izzy. And Sam. And Mrs. Gibson. Because of Delilah."

"Oh. Right," said her father. "But are you telling me Sam and Dotty were here when it happened?"

"Yes. But it wasn't my fault. I didn't want them staring at him. I just wanted them to go away, leave me alone. But he was too heavy for me to carry, so Izzy had to help me."

"*I* could have carried him," said Jason.

"They saw the whole thing?" Mr. Forbes asked.

"And afterward he kept coming to and going under and he was so weak." Brooke could feel the words shoving and jostling each other. "He could barely speak or move and he couldn't remember anything. *Anything!*" She stopped. The words were all out. She'd come to the end of it. There was nothing more to tell. Brooke raised her eyes and looked at them. It was their turn.

"Now what do we say?" Mr. Forbes looked at his wife. Mrs. Forbes made a helpless gesture. "It will be all over town."

Brooke stared stupidly at him. What was the matter with him? She was talking about Benji. Benji was the point, but he was talking about something else. It was like one of Jason's instant games, like figgerball, only worse. "What?" she wanted to scream it. "What will be all over town?"

The telephone shrilled in the hall.

For a moment Mr. Forbes's eyes scrambled as if he were looking for a loophole in his thoughts, and then they leveled again. "Answer that, Jason," he said. "Take a message. Tell them we're not home."

It *was* a game, Brooke realized suddenly, but not like figgerball at all. This game had a point. Hide! But why?

"It's the doctor," reported Jason. His hand covered the mouthpiece of the receiver. "For Brooke."

"I called him," Brooke said.

"*I'll* speak to him," said her mother.

She took the phone from Jason and disappeared with it into the front hall. "I'm sorry to bother you this late, but Benji. . . ." Her voice dropped out of hearing.

It was the game, again. I can go on playing, thought Brooke. I can teeter on this edge. In the dark. It's safer. Or I can move. She found herself standing in the hall before she remembered having left the kitchen. Mrs. Forbes glanced over her shoulder and waved her away. Brooke shook her head. Her mother turned her back and headed toward the dining room. Brooke cut in front of her, blocking her path.

Her mother lowered the phone. "Please, Brooke, I have to talk to the doctor."

"So talk," Brooke said.

Their eyes locked. Out of the receiver came a questioning tiny cartoonlike voice. They both heard it. Her mother lifted the phone again.

"Yes, I'm still here. . . . No, I wasn't home, but from what I can gather, there were a few added elements. . . . Right, in June. . . . Yes, that crossed my mind, too. . . . Yes, he's been taking them. . . . Yes. Both of them. Every day. . . . The hospital? Now?" Her voice rose. "Oh, I misunderstood." Her voice went flat again. "Tomorrow afternoon is fine. . . . Two o'clock. . . . Okay, I'll meet you there. And thank you for calling." She hung up.

"What is it? I want to know," demanded Brooke. "I have to."

"Let us handle this, Brooke." Her father had the bowl of ice cubes in his hand.

"Handle what?" Brooke snapped at him. "What is it?"

Her mother was still holding on to the telephone. "Calm down," she said.

"Tell me!"

Her mother and father exchanged glances again. "It's not that easy," said her father. "It's late and you've had a long day."

Forget this, thought Brooke. "Jason." She looked past them. "Can I borrow your jacket?"

"My army jacket!" said Jason.

"Where do you think you're going?" asked her father.

"To the doctor's!"

"Oh, no, you're not! You're not going anywhere!"

"Want me to come with you?" asked Jason.

"Please, Brooke," her mother said. She reached out a restraining hand. Brooke knocked it away. "This is crazy, Allen," said Mrs. Forbes. "It's gone too far."

"I don't know. I don't know," said Mr. Forbes.

"Look at us," Mrs. Forbes said. "Trapped in this hallway. Pitted against each other. I can't stand it!"

"What am I supposed to do?"

Mrs. Forbes hesitated. "Nothing could be worse than this," she said finally. "You've got to tell them."

There was no sound in the hall. The stillness stretched to a knotted silence.

"Okay," said Mr. Forbes at last. "Okay. But first I'm going to make myself a drink."

"Give me the bowl," said Mrs. Forbes. She took it out of his hands. "Sit down, Brooke, and soak your finger in this," she said. "It must hurt like the dickens."

Brooke cradled the bowl in her lap. Jason unzipped his jacket and settled on the step above her, hunched forward as if the stairs were bleachers. Mrs. Forbes braced herself against the hall table and crossed her ankles. She stared down at her feet.

Mr. Forbes came out of the kitchen and positioned himself on the square of oriental rug, a glass filled with pale brown liquid in his hand. Brooke saw his face in profile above the bulk of his shoulder and the heavy line of his arm. He cleared his throat.

"Look. Before I start, this isn't to go any further than these four walls. Is that clear?" He seemed to be talking to a place behind Mrs. Forbes's head. "Your mother and I have done our level best to keep this thing under wraps, and we're not going to change the game plan now. No one's found out and no one's going to find out. Understood?"

"Okay, Dad," said Jason.

Brooke nodded impatiently, staring at him hard, trying to speed him up.

"Okay," said Mr. Forbes. "That's point number one. Point number two is that Benji's going to outgrow this thing. He's going to outgrow it. There's no reason to believe he won't. After all, seventy percent of them do."

"Outgrow what?" Brooke's finger burned in the ice. "Who's them?"

"Kids like him who show signs of it early. He's going to be as normal as any other boy and I won't permit this thing to haunt him. I just won't."

It's gobbledegook, thought Brooke. I still don't know anything.

"I want him to have the same chances that you have," her father went on, "the same choices, without worrying that someone's going to muck around in his file like they did with that vice-presidential candidate a few years ago. I won't have Benji branded like that."

"Branded like what?" Brooke exploded. "What? Just say it!"

"Because of these motor seizures he has."

Huh? thought Brooke. There was a scrape of wood against the floor. Brooke turned toward her mother. Mrs. Forbes had pushed away from the table.

"He has epilepsy. What can I tell you," she said.

"Oh, no!" said Brooke.

"Epilepsy," repeated Mrs. Forbes. "That's what it's called."

Brooke felt sick. What did she know about epilepsy? Something dark and terrifying rose in her mind. Epilepsy. Benji. She shook her head, trying to get away from it, trying to get rid of it. Poor Benji. What would happen to him?

"You mean he's going to be a spastic basket case?" she heard Jason ask.

"Good heavens, no!" exclaimed Mr. Forbes. "You see, Marcie, you see how people react!"

"It's his brain, isn't it?" said Brooke. Through her shirt she could feel the side of the bowl, cold and damp against her stomach. "There's something wrong with it, something growing in it?"

"It's nothing like that," her mother said. "Don't look so scared. It is in his brain, but he's not going to die. He's not even sick."

"How can you say that?" asked Brooke. "You just said he had epilepsy."

"He does," answered her mother, "but it isn't going to hurt him. Let me see. How did the doctor explain it —"

"Basically, it's like an electrical overload," her father interrupted. "Every now and then, some of his nerve cells get overcharged and send out too much electricity. Then he short-circuits. Has a seizure. Like tonight. But all the rest of the time he's fine, absolutely fine."

Fine, thought Brooke. How could he be fine? She remembered him twisting on the kitchen floor, not hearing, not seeing.

Her mother seemed to read her mind. "I know that's hard for you to believe," she said. "His seizures still scare me even though I know what they are — it's true, Allen, they do — so it must have been doubly scary for you. But Brooke, I promise you the worst thing about epilepsy is the way it looks, not what it is. It's like ... ah, I know, it's like nightmares. They're horrible, but when you wake up they're over. Or a nosebleed. It's like a sudden nosebleed."

"Or a trick knee," added Mr. Forbes. "One minute you're standing and the next minute," he snapped his fingers, "you're on the ground and you don't know what hit you."

"Jud Hall has a knee like that," said Jason. "The coach has to pop it back into place."

"And then he's off and running again. Right?" said his father.

Jason nodded. "And now he gets to wear the Ace bandage every game."

"Epilepsy is really no worse than that," said Mrs. Forbes.

"Yes, but why does he have it at all?" protested Brooke. "Is he too smart?"

"It has nothing to do with intelligence," answered her mother. "The doctor told us that occasionally they can trace it to brain damage, or a head injury or even a high fever. Benji's had none of those. In his case, as in most cases, it just happens. They're not sure why. It's a mystery."

"Did I have it?" asked Jason.

"It doesn't run in families," answered his mother.

"Will I get it?"

"No. Of course not. It's *not* contagious," said his father.

"What's the big deal, then?" asked Jason. "It doesn't sound all that bad."

"It isn't," said his mother.

It couldn't be that simple, thought Brooke. Benji, gone away, his body jerking; then struggling up the stairs with him, Izzy grappling with his legs, trying to help. And after that, wiping him off with a washcloth. There was more to it. There had to be.

The ice was melting in the bowl. Brooke stirred the cubes with her finger, but the dark thing was still leeched to her mind. She glanced at her mother warily. "But it looks so awful," she said.

"I know," said her mother, "but not all seizures do." Mr. Forbes began to move restlessly in a slow, tight circle. "They differ. Sometimes they're over in a blink of an eye. Sometimes the person just goes rigid for a moment or two, sometimes — well, there's no set pattern for them. Even Benji's." Mrs. Forbes rested an arm on the curl of the banister. "But, Brooke, listen: no matter what kind of seizure it is, the important thing to remember, what you must understand, is that it doesn't damage him. It doesn't change him one iota."

"Then, why didn't you tell me before?" Brooke asked. "Why all this secrecy?"

"We didn't want to take the chance of

it slipping out," her father said. "By mistake," he added.

"You don't trust me."

"It isn't that," explained her mother. "We just figured you didn't need that kind of worry."

"But if you'd told me, I would have known what to do."

"There's nothing *to* do," said her mother, "except stand back and let the seizure run its course. That's about it, unless there are hard objects that ought to be moved out of his way. Things he might bang into. But I wish —" her mother made a rueful face — "I wish now that I *had* told you. Then you would have known that clenching his teeth is part of it and you would never, never have tried to stick your fingers in his mouth. As it was, you were the only one who got hurt."

Brooke leaned toward her mother and her mother bent down awkwardly and cradled her head for a moment. Tears stung Brooke's eyelids.

"And I wouldn't have been so frightened," she said. "And I could have told Izzy."

"No!" said her father. He stopped circling and faced them. "Not Izzy! Not anyone! Haven't you heard a word I've said?"

"Yes," said Brooke, "but Mom said it was okay."

"She's right," said her father grimly, "but that's not what the world thinks. That's the whole problem. What people turn it into. What they think it is. You name it, they think it. Everything from insanity to possessed by the devil. If people knew about Benji, they'd make him a social pariah. An outcast. They'd watch him. The doctor said so."

"Explain, then!" demanded Brooke. Her father shook his head. Brooke appealed to her mother. "Then, make the doctor explain. It's his job to make people understand."

"It doesn't work that way," said his father. "Believe me, Brooke, I've read things. All anyone needs to hear is the word and Benji is labeled. Labels stick. You have no idea what that means. It will be on his record for life." Her father coughed and his hand jerked. Liquid sloshed over the rim of his glass, wetting his wrist. He didn't seem to notice. "Even when he's outgrown it, when he's seizure-free, if it's on his record, they'll dig it up. It's crazy, I know, but he might not be able to get a job or a driver's license. Do what he wants to do."

"It *is* getting better, Allen," said Mrs. Forbes. "Laws are changing, people are learning."

"Not fast enough," said Mr. Forbes.

"And I won't risk it. I won't risk my boy." His voice cracked. He's going to cry, thought Brooke. Oh, no, he's going to cry. She couldn't believe it.

Her father crouched down. He set his glass on the rug and lowered his head. Brooke was afraid to move. She stared at the spiraling pattern of his hair. His hair is just like Benji's, she realized all of a sudden. It grows the same way. She felt Jason's knees move against her back.

Her father cleared his throat and looked up. "So we're going to wait it out. Buy time. Until he outgrows it." His voice was hoarse. "It was a judgment call on my part. It may not be perfect, but it was the best your mother and I could come up with. And now that you know, you can help us."

"What do you want us to do, Dad?" asked Jason.

"Protect him, remind him to take his pills, so this won't happen again."

"But they're not working," Brooke said to him. "He's been taking them and they're not working," she repeated to her mother. "You said they would, but they aren't."

Her mother fingered the top button on her shirt. "They will. They will," she said. "It's simply a matter of figuring out the proper combination, the correct dose for him. That's why we're going to the hospital

197

tomorrow, for more tests. Medically, they've made huge strides. We're really so lucky. They can almost always control it."

"*Almost always*," thought Brooke. Which was Benji? *Almost* or *always*?

"What if they can't?" she asked. "What if he doesn't outgrow it?"

"He's going to," said her father.

"But what if —"

"If he doesn't, he doesn't," interrupted her mother. "It's not the end of the world."

"If we have to, we'll deal with it," her father said. His voice was back to normal. "Meanwhile, we've got a lot going for us. All we have to do is stick together. Teamwork. That's the key." He tried a grin on her. "Hey, how's that finger?"

"Numb," said Brooke. "I think I've had it with the ice."

"Here." Her father leaned forward, reaching for the bowl. His knee went down, knocking over his drink.

"Never mind." Mrs. Forbes put a hand on his shoulder. "That's the nice thing about oriental rugs. Spots blend in."

Brooke heard Jason's stomach gurgle. "I need grub," he said. She could feel him stretching and flexing. "A little steak. Protein."

Brooke got to her feet slowly and picked up her father's glass. In the kitchen Mr. Forbes put the broom back in the closet and removed the bottle of brandy. Mrs. Forbes emptied the ashtray into the garbage and wiped the table with a sponge. As they moved by and around each other, clearing away traces, Brooke was lulled by small sounds: the splash of water in the sink, the swish of the mop, cupboard doors opening and closing, the clink of dishes. Jason settled for two bowls of cornflakes and Mr. Forbes swabbed Brooke's finger with antiseptic and bandaged it for her.

"The skin isn't broken." He gave her a quick hug. "But if it keeps you awake tonight, come and get me."

"What are you going to tell Benji?" she asked.

"Nothing," said her father. "He doesn't need to know."

"He's only six," her mother added. "He wouldn't understand."

"That's dubious, Mom," said Jason. "Dubious."

Brooke stared at him in surprise. There was milk and a cornflake on his chin.

"Benji knows he does something already," Jason said. "He just doesn't know what it is."

"They never remember any of the details," her mother said.

"I think it frightens him," said Brooke. "I think he's avoiding people."

"That will all clear up," said her father, "when he goes back to school."

School. Wait 'til they find out he isn't planning to go back to school, thought Brooke. I should tell them. But not now. I'm too tired. Tomorrow.

"What'll I tell Izzy?" she asked.

"We'll think of something," Mr. Forbes said. "Now, off to bed with you, kids. Your mother and I will finish up here."

Jason climbed the stairs ahead of Brooke. When he reached the hallway he hesitated and then stopped. They stood together outside Benji's door. Jason shifted his feet. Brooke couldn't think of anything to say. Finally Jason held up the trophy.

"Look, Brooke," he said. "Isn't that just incredible?"

Brooke looked. It was a mostly plastic stand, white and fakey marble. Perched on top was a small, gold-painted figure of a soccer player. The gold will probably turn black, Brooke thought, or peel off.

"Yes," she said. "It's incredible."

They studied it solemnly.

"I think I'll put it by Benji's bed," said Jason after a moment. "Where he can see it first thing. I might even loan it to him for a while."

"Okay. See you tomorrow."

"Okay. See you."

"Night."

"Night."

Brooke watched Jason turn the handle of Benji's door and tiptoe into his room.

The bathroom smelled as if Benji had forgotten to flush the toilet again. His underpants and bluejeans and the washcloth were still in the bathtub where she'd dumped them. Oh, well, they could wait. And so could Lucifur. He'd had plenty to eat. He could last until morning.

Epilepsy. Brooke stared into the mirror above the sink. "Epilepsy," she said aloud. The word sounded strange and a little foreign. I guess I'll get used to it, she thought.

The telephone rang. Someone else can get it, thought Brooke. I'm not doing any more tonight. Someone finally picked it up.

"Oh, Dotty," she heard her mother say. "How *are* you? How *is* she?"

I don't want to hear, Brooke said to herself. I don't want to know. She picked up her toothbrush and turned on the water full force.

Chapter 19

Lights played on the ceiling of Brooke's room. It was odd, she thought, still half asleep. But pretty. Like light refracted through a glass wind chime, or someone tilting mirrors, sending signals in yellow and orange and red. A magic show, just for her. There were noises, too, snapping sounds as if someone were breaking branches for kindling. Maybe Dr. Blazer's back, she thought. Maybe he's out there in the dark doing yard work again.

Brooke heard the sound of a car starting, the clutch-bang of shifting gears. Then a series of crackles, like strings of firecrackers popping outside her window. There was too much noise. Light leaped and licked across the ceiling. There was too much movement. Too much light. Fire! Something's on fire. The house! The thought shot her out of bed.

Now she smelled the smoke. Below her window the roof of the porch was dark and solid, but beyond the lilac hedge there were flames, climbing and curling up the walls of Dr. Blazer's barn. A cloud of black and gray smoke roiled above the flames, obscuring the top of the barn and blotting out the night sky.

Brooke wrestled with her doorknob and fled down the hall to her parents' room. She battered at their door.

"Mom! Dad! Wake up!"

Her father appeared in his pajama bottoms. Behind him, her mother tugged at the twisted top of her nightgown.

"Fire, Dad! There's a fire!"

"Noah's barn. It's burning up!" Benji stood at the other end of the hallway. Epilepsy. It was all Brooke could remember about him. He's got epilepsy.

"Marcie, get on the horn to Mike Banuchi," ordered Mr. Forbes.

"But you're fire captain," Brooke said.

"He'll know what to do." Mr. Forbes brushed past her.

"What's up?" Jason stumbled out of his room in his underwear, his face swollen with sleep. Brooke heard her mother dialing.

"Jason!" Mr. Forbes was back. "Get dressed. You, too, Brooke. Wear your jackboots. And hurry! Everything's dry as tinder out there and the water pressure's down."

Brooke's white painter's overalls hung over the back of her rocking chair. She stuck one leg in and hopped to the window. The black cloud had spread into a series of thick billows and the flames had reached the eaves. White smoke puffed out of the hayloft window.

Running footsteps passed her door. The other leg of her pants was inside out. Brooke tried to force her foot through. Suddenly the outside light high on the corner of the barn began to flicker. Brooke turned away from the window and searched the floor of her closet for her boots. As she laced them she felt something lumpy press into her side right above her hip. Benji's dinosaur.

She dashed down the back stairs and out by the garden. The garage doors were open and all the lights were on. Jason, in his army jacket, rounded the corner of the house hauling the garden hose. Brooke almost collided with him.

"Quick! Unscrew the nozzle," ordered Mr. Forbes. He dropped another length of hose onto the driveway. "Brooke, man the faucet, but don't turn it on 'til I yell." He was already screwing the hoses together.

Brooke put a hand on the cool metal

handle of the outdoor spigot and stood by. Flames spurted high above the lilac hedge, amazingly orange, brighter than pumpkin orange, brighter than any orange Brooke had ever seen. It was like looking into the sun. She saw her father and Jason, linked by the hose, crash through the hedge, the hose uncoiling on the driveway behind them.

"Now!" yelled her father. Brooke turned the faucet on as far as it would go. The water hissed and spat and a fine spray covered her hand.

"Brooke!" her father yelled again.

"It's coming!" Brooke yelled back.

The screen door slammed and Benji appeared on the stoop lugging the yellow plastic bucket from under the kitchen sink. Holding the handle with both hands, he struggled down the steps, the bucket bumping off his knees. Water sloshed over the side.

Brooke watched him put the bucket down and rub his hands against his legs. Epilepsy, she thought. He picked up the bucket again and she watched him trudge, canted backward, toward the break in the hedge. He paused on the lit patch of driveway. It was as if Brooke had never seen him before, as if his small, solitary outline and the elongated shadow cast by his legs were only a bridge between light and dark. Then he set off again, doggedly, and she saw that he was just Benji; her old Benji, she thought, on a mission.

She reached him at the hedge and grabbed onto the bucket. A wave of heat hit her. Jason came crashing back through the gap in the bushes.

"Towels," he panted, "the big ones. And wet them. Sparks are landing on Blazer's house and the hose won't reach. I'm getting the ladder."

"C'mon, Benji," said Brooke. "Leave the bucket."

"I thought it would be good," Benji said.

Mrs. Forbes ran past them wearing a raincoat over her nightgown and carrying a fire extinguisher in each hand. She looked scared. "I've got to spray the garage," she said. "The fire's too close."

The patterned swimming towels were in the laundry room, folded on top of the dryer. Brooke dumped them into the sink and turned on the water.

"Can I carry them?" Benji held out his arms. Brooke looked down at him. His pajama bottoms were soaked and clinging to his legs. "I couldn't find my bluejeans," he explained.

The sopping towels dripped along the floor. "Your shoelaces are untied," warned Brooke.

Outside, pieces of ash floated around them like lint shaken from the blanketed sky. They saw the thin white line of water from the garden hose arch into the flames.

"Bet Dad can save it," said Benji. Then he halted and squinted upward. Bats flitted over their heads and more bats zigzagged erratically above the garage roof. "They're trying to get home," Benji said. "I'm glad Lucifur's upstairs."

His words were almost lost in the whoosh and crackle of the blaze. A gust of hot wind blew against them and claws of flame reached over the hedge toward the garage.

From far away, through the roar of the fire, Brooke heard the faint, insistent clanging of a bell. Help was coming.

The barn was gone. In the morning light everything seemed altered to Brooke. Where the barn had been there was now only empty space, and Brooke could suddenly see distances that the barn had blocked, all the way to the tall maples lining the next street, and the parked cars, and even beyond them to the openness of the fairground.

The sour smell of wet ashes hung in the air.

Mike Banuchi paced the perimeter of the charred and smoking ruins in his heavy boots, turning over shovelfuls of ash or prodding at what remained of a beam. The fire still smoldered. Water from the last of the hoses continued to play over the site, damping it down. Occasionally there was a hiss and a jet of steam.

The paint on the side of Dr. Blazer's house was blistered and the windows were streaked with water. Jason was on the roof collecting the swimming towels and tossing them down to Izzy. The Superman towel caught on the gutter and hung there, sodden and bedraggled.

People were all over Dr. Blazer's back-yard and his lawn. A few drifted toward their parked cars, but most of the rest stood around as if they planned to make a morning of it. Some of them had even brought camp stools and blankets. Half the town must be here, thought Brooke. She watched Mr. Pritchard shoo Ricky Renwick off the hood of the fire engine and then climb aboard himself and start to rewind one of the hoses onto the big drum.

Benji's hand slipped into hers. His eyes looked enormous, the shadows under them even darker than usual, as if he'd been rubbing his eyes with sooty fists.

"Are you okay?" Brooke asked him. Benji turned and wiped the side of his face and his nose on the part of her tee shirt that hung out of her overalls.

"Poor Noah," he said. "He'll be sad. It's gone."

Brooke remembered the end of it, like building the barn backward, the last moments when everything had been stripped away until only the post-and-beam frame still held out stubbornly against the yellow flames.

"They saved his house," she said. And our garage, she thought. But it had been a close call. The section of lilac hedge between the garage and the barn was gray and shriveled.

"The experiment's gone, too," said Benji. He swayed against her and for a second Brooke wondered whether he was going to go down again.

Her father and mother wended their way through the crowd. Mrs. Forbes had changed out of her nightgown into a pair of bluejeans. Mr. Forbes had an arm around her. "How are you guys holding up?" he asked, ruffling the top of Benji's head with his free hand. "You were terrific."

"I'm going in to make gallons of coffee," said Mrs. Forbes. "I wish I had doughnuts or something to go with it."

"There are some coffee cakes in the freezer," Brooke reminded her. "Unless Jason's found them."

"Benji," said Mr. Forbes, "want to give me a hand? We're going to need another shovel and that heavy rake." Brooke felt Benji's hand slip away.

"Hey, Brooke! I have a present for you," shouted Izzy. She dropped a mound of towels on Brooke's feet.

"Thanks a bundle."

"Where's Benji?" Izzy lowered her voice. "I saw him a while ago."

"With Dad."

"Is he all right?" Izzy was whispering.

"Yes," Brooke said. "Basically. But I can't talk now."

"Later?" Sweat and heat had turned Izzy's hair into a wild tangle of curls.

Brooke nodded.

"Okay," said Izzy. "Whenever." Brooke smiled at her and Izzy smiled back. I wish my hair curled like that, thought Brooke. She ought to wear it that way all the time. "I know it sounds gruesome," Izzy was whispering again, "but this is sort of neat. Jason said the sparks were flying everywhere and he's got huge burn holes in his army jacket. He says —"

"Brooke!" Mike clumped over to them. His eyes were rimmed with red. "I need your dad."

"Want me to get Jason?" offered Izzy.

Mike shook his head. "Weirdest thing," he muttered. "Doesn't make sense."

"I know," said Brooke. "It went up so fast."

"Yeah. Too fast, and from the outside in." Mike seemed to be debating with himself. "And there's a kerosene can I can't explain."

"What kerosene can?" asked Izzy sharply. "Where?"

A question formed in Brooke's mind, but she didn't want to ask it. She stalled, willing herself stupid.

"You mean someone set it?" Izzy asked for her.

"I mean I don't like the looks of it," Mike told her. "That's all I'm saying."

"On purpose?" persisted Izzy.

"Brooke's dad'll know," Mike said.

"He's in the garage," said Brooke.

"Arson! Did you hear that, Brooke?" Izzy's eyes glowed with excitement. "I'll bet it was Dr. Blazer."

The fire had almost jumped the hedge. If the wind had been stronger. . . . Brooke thought. If the barn had been closer. . . .

"He isn't even here," she said.

"Remote control," said Izzy.

Mr. Banuchi and Mr. Pritchard crouched close together on the singed grass. Brooke saw her father and Mike join them. There was the sound of cars starting up and someone yelling. "Renwick! Hey, Renwick! Move your truck. It's blocking traffic."

"I'm going to tell Jason," said Izzy. Jason was still on the roof, high above everyone, scuffing about as if fire lurked beneath every shingle. Izzy darted off.

Threes, Brooke thought. Things come in threes. That's what Mom always says. Delilah, Benji, the barn. Three.

Izzy was climbing the ladder that leaned against Dr. Blazer's house. She was only on the third rung but already she was peering down at the ground and clinging to the ladder like a fly. She'll never make it, thought Brooke. I'd better go help her.

Then she heard a noise that made her stop and stare past the fire engine to Ashpotag Road. She stood absolutely still, listening. The sound came again, a clutch-bang, the same sound she had last heard lying in bed watching the flame lights on her ceiling. An old, familiar sound that was suddenly new and frightening.

Not threes, Brooke thought. Fours.

Chapter 20

A car parked next to Dr. Blazer's mailbox pulled out and Brooke watched Sam's truck back into the space. The front wheels straightened. The clutch banged again and then the motor died. Sam climbed down and strolled across the lawn. His thumbs were hooked into his belt. Brooke couldn't take her eyes off him.

Benji crossed her line of vision dragging the heavy rake, metal prongs up. A group had formed around Mike and Mr. Forbes. Brooke saw her father kneel down. Whispers rustled through the crowd and clusters of people shifted and reformed.

Sam moved slower, sticking close to the wall of Dr. Blazer's house. Brooke saw him stop and look and then step out a bit, wiping at the top of his head. Water still dripped from the eaves.

Her father and Mike were coming toward her now, walking the burn line, Mike

talking and gesturing and her father
listening intently. They seemed to pull
people along with them, Mr. Pritchard
and Mr. Banuchi and the man from the
Cut-Rate Drugstore and Mrs. Banuchi in
her wraparound housedress, the one with
the black-eyed Susans all over it that Izzy
hated. Benji trotted along with them, a
little apart, towing the rake.

Sam watched them.

Brooke saw everything, singly and together, as if through opposite ends of a
telescope. She saw Ricky Renwick and
Jud Hall sneak back onto the fire engine.
Jud played driver and Ricky toyed with
the bell. She saw Sam run his forearm
across his face, under his nose, and then
hook his thumbs back into his belt. She
saw her father nodding at Mike and she
saw Mike stop talking and then she saw
them both turn and scan the crowd. She
saw the flash of Izzy's hair.

"Who in the world would do a thing like
that?" she heard Mr. Pritchard ask.
Brooke's heart was pounding. She looked
away from Sam, feeling herself prickle hot
and cold.

"With everything so dry, the whole
block could have gone," someone added.

"Hope this doesn't mean we're in for a
rash of barn burnings," Mike said.

"Couldn't have been for the insurance,"

said Mrs. Banuchi. "Nothing in that barn but bats."

"Worth more standing," agreed Mr. Forbes. "People pay an arm and a leg for old beams and weathered siding. I know."

"Kids, maybe," suggested the man from the drugstore. "For kicks."

The bell on the fire engine clanged.

"I didn't do it," said Ricky.

Everyone was looking at them.

"Don't look at me," yelled Jud. "It was him."

"Funny idea of kicks," growled Mr. Pritchard.

Should I tell, thought Brooke. Tell Dad?

Suddenly Sam spoke. His voice stunned her. It was the last voice she expected to hear.

"Don't blame the kids," he said. "Just thank your lucky stars that barn's gone."

Sam's neck and face and the top of his bald head were flushed red. How is he going to tell it? Brooke thought. She couldn't look at him. It was too embarrassing. She stared at the patch of grass in front of her, wishing she were someplace else.

"I don't care who did it or why," Sam's voice boomed in her ears. "This town owes them a vote of thanks. I would have done it myself" — he paused — "if I'd thought of it."

What is he doing? wondered Brooke.

He's not telling. He's not telling at all. He's turning everything around, upside down.

"Are you out of your mind, Sam!" exclaimed Mr. Forbes. "Have you any idea what you're saying?"

"You bet I do!" said Sam. "I'm glad it's gone. That barn's been a breeding ground for years. I've said so time and again but none of you would listen. You all ignored me. And now even with it down it may be too late. They already got to your boy and I hate to think how many others!"

Benji! So that was it. Brooke had heard enough. She understood. There were questions and exclamations from the people around her, but she didn't wait to hear Sam's answers. By the time she reached Benji, she didn't hear anything at all. A white cone of silence seemed to enclose them both.

"Come on, Benj." She spoke gently so as not to startle him. "It's time to go."

He looked up at her. "Where?" His face was streaked where sweat had dripped from his hair.

"Home," Brooke told him. She grasped him under the arms. "Drop the rake. Okay?" She expected him to be heavy, the way he'd been before, on the stairs, but he came up easily onto her hip. She could run.

Her father was in her way. His voice broke through to her. "You're way out of line, Sam. Go home and sleep it off," he said.

"Too late for that!" said Sam. "Rosie told me about that time in school, but I didn't put two and two together until I saw it with my own eyes. In your kitchen. Last night!"

"Shut up, Sam!" Mr. Forbes's voice was icy. "You don't know what you're talking about!"

"I wish I didn't," Sam shot back, "but I was there! And I've got children of my own to protect. We all do!"

Brooke felt Benji's ribs against her chest. His legs tightened around her waist.

"Get out of here, Sam!" commanded her father. "Before I really lose my temper." The crowd had parted. There was no one between them and Sam.

"Protect them from what?" somebody asked.

"The bats! That's what I've been telling you. They've gotten to the Forbes boy. They've contaminated him. He's sick. My guess is rabies, or worse. He could be a carrier, for all we know."

"Dad!" said Brooke urgently. She touched the sleeve of his shirt. A muscle twitched in his cheek. She waited, but he didn't speak. He can't, she realized suddenly. He can't get the words out.

Benji was whispering into her ear. "Is that what I have, Brooke?" he asked. His voice sounded sad. Brooke shook her head, hugging him hard. His cheek pressed against hers. "Am I going to die?"

"No!" Brooke gave him a last hug and put him down. She had to be quick and very clear. It no longer mattered who heard. "Listen, Benji." She crouched until they were eye to eye. "You've got —" Pick one, she thought, pick one. "What you've got is like having nosebleeds, every now and then, for no reason. Nosebleeds look yucky, but then they stop and you're fine. Your thing is called epilepsy. Okay? It's different, but it's the same. Yucky-looking, but you're fine. Okay?" There was a gasp from someone. Brooke ignored it.

Did he understand? She searched his face for a clue.

"School," he said.

"Yes," said Brooke. "School and everything. Okay?"

Benji nodded. Brooke stood up. She wished it were over, but it wasn't and, worse than that, there was only one way out. She hated to go there, but she had to. Holding Benji's hand, she advanced on Sam. I'll tell on you, she thought, if I have to.

She heard a low "How dreadful!"

"The poor mother."

Brooke didn't recognize that voice either. She could feel eyes on her, but she kept her eyes on Sam.

"Benji has epilepsy," she said. "Not rabies. Epilepsy."

Sam stepped back, his mouth half open. "Good Lord! You mean bats spread that, too?"

"They couldn't spread it even if they wanted to," Brooke said. "Epilepsy is unspreadable. Benji could cough on you or sneeze on you or spit on you or bite you and you wouldn't get it. Go ahead, Benji, touch him!"

There was movement somewhere in the crowd. Brooke swung around, ready for anything, daring anyone to shrink away.

"Well, what do you know about that!" It was Mrs. Banuchi in her flowered housedress. She plowed to the front like a bulldozer wrapped in birthday paper. "A nosebleed. I never thought of epilepsy that way, but it figures. Scares you half to death and hardly amounts to a hill of beans."

"Hill of beans! Who are you kidding?" demanded Sam. "She didn't see it," he went on, "and my Rosie's in his class."

"I have seen it," answered Mrs. Banuchi. "I grew up with it. My sister has it." She tapped Benji on the shoulder. "Izzy's aunt."

"Not the one with all the children?" Mrs. Pritchard asked her.

"That's the one," said Mrs. Banuchi. "She has epilepsy. It's a damn nuisance, but it never slowed *her* down any. Six children, a whiner for a husband, and runs the gas station in Biloxi."

"The one who was here over Christmas and brought that wonderful tomato chutney?" Mrs. Pritchard still sounded doubtful.

"That's Lulu," said Mrs. Banuchi.

"She seemed perfectly normal to me," said Mr. Pritchard.

"She is and so is Benji, here. Look at him. Pants too short and filthy dirty, like any other boy."

"I don't buy that," growled Sam. "How come you're only telling us about her now? If your sister's so all-fired normal, how come you never told us about her before?"

"Why should I?" asked Mrs. Banuchi. "You may enjoy discussing other people's hay fever and hemorrhoids and back problems, but I don't. Besides, it's her business. Period!"

"Don't listen to her," Sam insisted. "There's more to it than that. I've got evidence. How are you going to explain the dog?" he asked Mrs. Banuchi. "That dog of Dotty's?"

"What about her?" asked Mrs. Banuchi.

"I took her to the vet's myself and believe me, she was a goner! Half paralyzed already and foaming at the mouth."

There was a silence. That's true, thought Brooke. That's exactly what she looked like.

"Don't tell me that wasn't rabies," Sam finished defiantly, "or this epilepsy business."

"It wasn't," Mr. Forbes spoke up from behind Brooke. "Dotty phoned us late last night. The dog was poisoned from eating those azalea bushes she planted. If you don't believe me, go ask my wife."

"Satisfied?" asked Mrs. Banuchi.

Sam's stomach sagged farther over his belt. Brooke saw him swallow. His Adam's apple bobbed up and down.

"That dog hasn't a brain in its head," announced Mr. Banuchi. "Last summer it ate all my geraniums and had weeks of diarrhea all over my —"

"No need to go into details," Mrs. Banuchi interrupted him. "Besides, I'm bushed. I've had enough excitement for one day."

"Mom's making coffee," offered Brooke.

"Just what I need," said Mrs. Banuchi, "and if you don't mind, I'm going to drink it on your front porch. You coming?" she asked Mrs. Pritchard.

"Well. . . ." Mrs. Pritchard hesitated. "If you say it's all right."

"You can sit in the hammock," Mrs. Banuchi told her. "I'd stretch it out. Coffee, everyone!" she called back over her shoulder.

For a moment nobody moved. People stared openly at Benji; some shifted their gaze when they caught Brooke's eye and pretended to be looking at something else. Two or three smiled at him. Then the crowd began to break up. Old Miss Griggs folded her camp stool. Mr. Pritchard picked up Benji's rake. A group of women and the man from the Cut-Rate Drugstore followed Mrs. Banuchi.

"I never knew anyone with epilepsy before," Brooke heard someone comment. Well, now you do, she thought.

Sam stared after them, the sun glinting off his bald head. Brooke hoped he wouldn't come to the house. She hoped he would just get into his truck and go away.

Benji's hand felt hot and sticky. She looked around for her father, wondering whether he was furious with her. He was closer than she expected, only a few steps away, but all she could see in his eyes was fatigue.

Her father closed the gap between them. He took hold of Benji's other hand. "Might be a good idea to change out of those pajama bottoms, old man," he said, and then he looked over Benji's head to Brooke. "I'm going to get a cup of coffee. What about you?"

Coffee? She'd never had more than a sip, it tasted so bitter. But maybe with cream and lots of sugar.

"Sure," she said.

They started toward the house swinging Benji between them. Then he let go of their hands and trotted on ahead. Brooke felt her father's arm across her shoulders, heavy, as if he were leaning on her. By the time they reached the lilac hedge she had matched her stride to his.

The last hose had been rewound onto the drum of the fire engine and Jud Hall was playing driver again. Only a cleanup crew still worked around Dr. Blazer's house. From her bedroom window Brooke watched Izzy and Mrs. Banuchi disappear down Ashpotag Road. Pieces of ash were caught in her window screen and a film of soot covered the sill. Brooke ran a finger through it.

She smelled coffee. Mom must be making another pot, she thought. Brooke closed both doors to her room and sat down in her rocking chair. She was glad to be alone. She tugged off her boots and rested her elbows on her knees. Her feet smelled and her clothes stuck to her. She flapped her shirt and then lifted her hair off her neck with her hands. It felt stiff and heavy with sweat. I'm too dirty to live. She groaned. I have to get out of these clothes and take a shower and wash my hair. She unhooked her overalls and stood up. Benji's dinosaur was still in her pocket. I'd better rescue it, she thought, before I forget and it disintegrates in the washing machine. Her overalls dropped around her ankles. Brooke sat back down and unwound the last of the matted toilet paper from around the dinosaur.

Bits of gray clay dust fell on her bare thighs. The tip of the dinosaur's tail was missing, but otherwise it seemed all right. The whole of its back was inlaid with triangular plates, and triangular spikes studded both sides. It's so perfect, marveled Brooke. How did he make those plates and spikes identical? They were all exactly alike. The same size, the same shape, as if they'd been stamped from a mold. Suddenly her mind registered what she was seeing. She sat unmoving, staring at the dinosaur in her hand. Of course. He hadn't made them at all. That's why they were perfect. They were his pills, straight from the bottle. Stuck in and painted gray. A whole summer's worth.

The little creep!

Her bathroom door opened and in he came. "Brooke!" he said. His mouth was working and he sounded worried. "My tooth. It's gone; I think I swallowed it."

His tooth! Who cared? Swallowing a baby tooth was nothing. I could knock all the rest of your teeth down your throat! she thought. It was what he hadn't swallowed. That was what mattered. Enough, maybe, to make the difference between *almost* and *always*.

"I love my dinosaur, Benji," Brooke said to him. She weighed it in her hand. She felt like throwing it at him. She felt like laughing. "There's just one little thing I want to ask you."

Chapter 21

Late Labor Day afternoon Brooke sat by
herself in the kitchen feeling a little sleepy
from all the corn she had eaten at the Fire-
men's Barbecue. On the table in front of
her was a pile of money, bills and some
change. She and Izzy had left the baseball
game early to settle accounts. Her share
came to $487.50.

Brooke looked down at it. It was serious
money. Not fun money. Not the kind you
could go crazy with at the penny-candy
store. There was too much of it. It made
her feel older, but apart.

She picked up the two quarters and
rubbed them idly between her fingers. I
think I'll buy a watch, she thought, with a
thin leather band and a small white face.
And definitely roman numerals. I need one
for school. A watch would be good to keep
track of where I'm supposed to be without
asking. The click of the quarters slipping

across each other was oddly pleasing, like metallic chirping.

Gradually she sensed that she was not alone. Someone was behind her, watching her. She could feel it. Brooke turned toward the door, wondering who it was and how long they'd been there.

A pink balloon three feet off the ground and trailing string hovered in the doorway like a small person. Brooke stared at it. The balloon dipped shyly, then sidled around the doorjamb and lingered, irresolute, close to the wall. Brooke waited to see if it would do anything else. The balloon wavered and then, very slowly, turned, revealing letters, one by one, like skywriting. H-A-P-P-Y B-I-R-T-H-D-A-Y R-O-S-I-E-! Having delivered the message, the balloon turned away again. It's run out of things to say, Brooke thought.

Benji's head appeared in the doorway and then he crawled into the kitchen, carrying a pair of scissors. The balloon scuttled a few feet along the wall. Benji followed it and snipped off a section of its string. The balloon rose slightly.

"I know what you're doing," said Brooke.

"Making it last," Benji said. "Until tomorrow."

"Are you all set to go?"

Benji sat back on his heels. "Yes. Rosie's going to try and get there early, before breakfast maybe, and save two desks. So I don't have to worry about that."

"I like Rosie," said Brooke, but she was thinking about Sam. She had been thinking about Sam and the fire on and off all week.

"She let me lick the icing off her candles. Seven candles."

"It sounds like a good party, but was it all okay? I mean, did anyone act funny around you?"

Benji was watching his balloon. "Mrs. Renwick made me have seconds on fried chicken," he said after a moment. "But Rosie ate it for me."

"What about Sam?"

"Sam? Well. . . ." Benji cleared his throat. "He sort of looked at me, the way he does. Like this." Benji ambled his eyes in Brooke's direction without moving his head.

"Did he do it the whole time?"

"I don't know. He asked me if it was okay for me to run, and then he made me captain of a relay team. And then there was the treasure hunt and my party bag with the miniature paint set and the little brush."

I can't protect him from Sam's watching, Brooke thought. Anyway, Benji was better about it than she was. He was *fine*. Maybe the best thing she could do now was to stop being one of the watchers. Stop trying to protect him. That kind of protecting could hurt. Mom and Dad had tried; and Sam had tried to protect the whole town, to be a hero, and look what had happened. She pictured Sam's worried Santa Claus face and suddenly she knew that, right or wrong, she was never going to tell about the clutch-bang. The time for telling had passed. The days had closed over it. And maybe it wasn't really Benji Sam was watching anymore. Maybe he was watching himself.

Benji came over to the table and picked up his new bottle of pills. The pills were new, too, not hard and triangular like the old ones, but soft and oval.

"I've conquered pills," he said. "Watch."

He worked up some saliva and then put one of the yellow-and-white capsules into his mouth. His neck stretched and his eyes widened. He looked surprised. He swallowed again.

"If Sam and Dad start rebuilding the barn right away, I'll bet they could get it all framed in before the first frost," Brooke said.

"The thing of it is," — Benji put the bottle of pills back on the table — "even if they rebuild it, the bats might not come back."

"Why wouldn't they?"

Benji gazed out of the kitchen window.

"They might not like a new barn." He cleared his throat. "If they don't come back, Noah might go away."

"Just because of the bats?"

"He likes bats best of all the animals he trained for the army. Better than pigeons. Even better than the pigs."

"He trained *pigs* for the *army?* That was his job?"

"Not just pigs. He trained all kinds of animals. I told you. For the army and the navy and the air force. Even for other countries and airports," Benji said. "Pigs are terrific smellers. Better than dogs. They can smell out bombs twelve inches underground. But people were too embarrassed to use them. Noah says people felt silly with a pig on a leash."

He tells Benji all this stuff, thought Brooke, and I've never even met him.

"But Noah says bats are the most interesting. Noah says we've hardly begun to learn what they already know." Benji turned away from the window. " 'Course, pigs are easier. It's okay to keep a pig."

The balloon nodded modestly by the door. Benji retrieved it and rubbed it up and down on the front of his shirt until the balloon was stuck to him with static. "Where's Dad?"

"The game must have gone into extra innings," answered Brooke.

"Where's Mom?"

"In the bindery. Where else?"

Benji left the kitchen.

"Hey! Wait a minute," Brooke called after him. "Tell me more about Dr. Blazer."

"I have to do something," he called back. "Something important. Meet me on the lawn."

Brooke stared out into the empty hall. Then she put the sugar bowl on top of her pile of money and stood up. She knew without asking what the something important was.

Outside, the air was still warm, but it was a thin kind of warmth with no weight to it. The sun had gone down, but the red leaves on the early-turning branch of the maple tree were so bright they looked as if sunlight were on them.

Delilah trotted up the driveway. A long green vine trailed out of her mouth and dragged behind her. She's hit the garden again, thought Brooke. Mom will have a fit. Oh, no, she won't. It's the squash plant that took over the compost heap. She could see the dark-yellow overgrown squash bumping along the driveway. Delilah made a smart left turn and, with her head up and tail high, disappeared down Ashpotag Road, towing her booty home. Dumb dog! Hadn't learned a thing.

Brooke glanced up at Benji's window. No one had noticed the missing screen and soon it wouldn't matter. It was almost time for storm windows. She waited for him by the maple tree.

When he came out of the house, he was wearing his silver gloves. He came carefully down the porch steps and across the lawn. His sneaker laces were untied, but Brooke decided not to tell him. Lucifur's head poked out above the rim of his cupped hands.

"What made you change your mind?" Brooke asked.

Benji blew gently on the back of Lucifur's head, parting the soft fur between his ears. "I didn't," he said, "but Noah says there are some animals you can't have. If you keep them, you kill them."

"Will he be all right on his own?"

"Yes," Benji said. "I remembered *fu*, the Chinese word for bat, and I remembered what else it means."

"Good luck and happiness," Brooke said. "Right?"

"There's a third thing. I'd forgotten, but now I've remembered. It means long life, too."

Lucifur chittered up at them.

I'm going to miss him, thought Brooke.

"Silly bat," said Benji. "Silly old bat."

He looked around, checking. Everything was still. A few red maple leaves lay on the grass at their feet, flat and perfect, as if they'd been painted there. Benji sniffed the air. Then he raised his arms. His open silver-gloved hands looked like a launching pad. Lucifur crouched there, his ears alert and scanning.

"Long life, Lucifur," Brooke said.

"Go on," Benji encouraged.

Lucifur spread his wings and took off. One second he was visible, a dark slash in the twilight; the next second he was gone.

Brooke searched the treeline, half expecting to see him come swooping back and land on Benji's collar, but he didn't. She hoped he knew where he was going and how to get there. Maybe, right now, while she was hoping, instinct was guiding him. She wondered what Benji was thinking. Was he wondering if Lucifur would find the others, and if he did and if the barn were rebuilt and if the bats came back in the spring, whether Lucifur would recognize him? Was he sad?

Benji sighed and pulled off his gloves. "I've been thinking," he said, "about a pig for my room."

"What?" He couldn't be serious. "I can't believe you, Benji!"

"A pig is okay. And I could train it. To

protect the house and things. A guard pig."

He *was* serious. But not a pig. "Not in your room, Benji."

"Why?"

"Because I've never even heard of anyone keeping a pig in his room. And how do you think you're going to train it? You don't know the first thing about pigs, Benji."

"First I'm going to housebreak it, and then —"

"Housebreak it! How do you do that?"

Benji stuffed the gloves deep into his back pocket.

"Let's go ask Noah."